'What did you

Cathy blushed, cor
indignant for a woman who was half out of
her bra.

'I saw everything.' Zack's lips grazed her tilted
chin, followed the line of her neck to her
delicate collarbone. 'I saw these.' He closed
both hands over her breasts, kneading until an
arousal nearly as hot as his own was radiating
from her in shimmering waves. *I saw you.*

She gave a deep sigh and leaned against him,
her body lax. 'Kiss me again,' she said,
parting her lips and cutting the last string of
his control.

With a groan, he covered her mouth with his
and ground his body against hers.

'I can't take this,' he said, wrenching away.
'Either we go home now or wind up flat on the
dirt floor.'

She glanced down, then lifted her gaze to his.
'I guess I'm too practical not to prefer a bed.'

He pressed his fingertips to her swollen lips.
'Then hold that thought,' he said, silently
thankful that he still had the Jaguar parked
outside.

*Zero to ninety in a matter of seconds sounded
almost fast enough…*

Dear Reader,

Remember your first crush? Maybe it was on Davy Jones or Kevin Bacon or Brad Pitt. And maybe it was on the cutest, most popular boy in the fifth grade…

Cathy Timmerman remembers her first crush, Zack Brody. And when she returns to the town where they first met, she learns that he's grown up even better than she'd imagined—in fact, the man is a legendary Romeo! It turns out that a group of Zack's old girlfriends are looking for a woman to give the 'Smooth Operator' a taste of his own medicine. Cathy—no longer the chubby social outcast—finds herself volunteered. But can she really seduce Zack…and then leave him? Especially when he's even better in person than in her dreams?

Happy reading!

Carrie Alexander

P.S. Please let me know if you liked Zack and Cathy. You can write to me care of Harlequin Books, 225 Duncan Mill Road, Don Mills, Ontario, M3B 3K9, Canada.

SMOOTH MOVES

by

Carrie Alexander

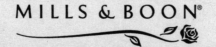

MILLS & BOON®

*MILLS & BOON and MILLS & BOON with the Rose Device
are registered trademarks of the publisher.*

*First published in Great Britain 2002
by Harlequin Mills & Boon Limited,
Eton House, 18-24 Paradise Road, Richmond, Surrey TW9 1SR*

© Carrie Alexander 2001

ISBN 0 263 83271 6

21-0502

*Printed and bound in Spain
by Litografia Rosés S.A., Barcelona*

Prologue

FOR SUCH AN ordinary middle-American town, Quimby had its share of legends. There was the ghost who haunted the clock tower of the old stone courthouse. There was Eunice LaSalle, the 1962 prom queen who'd gone to Hollywood and costarred in an Elvis beach flick. Reputedly, a monster muskie lived in Mirror Lake and nibbled on the toes—or various other bobbing appendages—of unwary skinny-dippers. And on one unforgettable night in 1985, the Quimby Kingpins had beaten the Buxton Bluejackets with a half-court lob at the buzzer, 53 to 52.

Then there was Heartbreak.

Zachary "Heartbreak" Brody, aka The Smooth Operator.

A man who was a legend in his own time, according to the female half of Quimby's populace.

And they would know.

As it happened, the five women who'd been most seriously "Heartbroken" gathered every Wednesday evening at Cathy Timmerman's arts and crafts shop. Scarborough Faire—formerly known as Kay's Krafts—was at 1208 Central Street, Quimby's version of Main Street, U.S.A. An innocent setting for the chicanery to come. Although, as it would turn out, appearances were decidedly deceiving.

The weekly meeting of the five women in question

was purported to be an informal craft class. Local ladies signed up left and right for Cathy's other classes, even woodburning and china painting, but the Wednesday-night calligraphers had closed their ranks to the unini-tiated. Group therapy hadn't been their initial intention, yet nearly every week the talk turned to Zack Brody: What he'd done to them, how they still hadn't recov-ered, where he was now, whose heart he was currently breaking with his deceptively charming and oh, so smooth and seductive ways.

Which was not to say that the five women hated the man. Goodness, no.

It was Zack's particular skill that he'd left even his jilted bride harboring certain feelings—definitely more than *fond*—for him. In fact, if the truth be known, several of the women maintained a secret fantasy that someday she would be the one to capture the legendary Lo-thario's heart for good. The likelihood that the rest of his perfect male specimen body would be included in the deal was...not unpleasant.

Be that as it may, there were also times, when the hour grew late and strong ink fumes had gone to their heads, that the five women bandied about a suitable revenge. 'Twas only fair, they said. Heartbreak should have a taste of his own medicine.

Thus, upon the fateful evening of Heartbreak Brody's prodigal return to Quimby, a scheme was afoot. A nefar-ious plot that would turn out to be neither as easy nor as simple as intended. But far more effective.

And it all began at Cathy Bell Timmerman's arts and crafts shop....

"YOU'LL NEVER GUESS," Gwendolyn Case boomed as she sailed through Scarborough Faire's aisles toward the long farmhouse table where the rest of the Wednesday-night calligraphers had already taken out their pens and papers. "Guess who's coming back to Quimby!"

Cathy Timmerman, the shopkeeper and head calligrapher, stifled her sigh of frustration. Calligraphy required concentration, hard to come by with this group.

Faith Fagan, a wan blonde, looked confused. "But you said we'd *never*—"

"Guess!" With one forceful word, buxom brunette Gwendolyn easily silenced meek Faith. Suffused with the power of her knowledge, Gwen put her hands on her hips and smiled broadly at the group. As self-appointed doyenne of the post office, she had her ear to the grapevine...and her mouth perpetually set to gossip mode.

Looking as peaked as Faith, Laurel Barnard slumped against the spindle back of one of the wooden chairs Cathy had picked up at rummage sales and then painted with colorful, whimsical patterns of swirls, dots, stripes and stars. Laurel, the pretty owner of the dress shop next door, opened her mouth, then couldn't seem to summon words. Only one man was legend enough to evince such an announcement.

"Heartbreak," said a calm voice.

Gwendolyn's head spun around. Air huffed through her open mouth.

Carefully Julia Knox lifted the point of her pen off the paper. She shook her head so that a misplaced strand of honey-brown hair fell neatly into place in her precision-cut bob. "Yes, ladies, it's shocking but true. Zack Brody is returning to Quimby."

Somewhat deflated now that she'd been beaten to the punch, Gwen plopped into a peppermint-striped chair. "Yeah. You're right."

Allie Spangler said, "Boy-oh-boy-oh-boy," and then suddenly all five of the Heartbroken were talking at once, even Faith.

Only Cathy Timmerman, whose position with the Wednesday nighters was often less that of a crafts teacher than a therapist, was silent. And it wasn't because she didn't know Zack "Heartbreak" Brody, although as far as these women and the rest of the town were concerned, she didn't. Never met him at all.

Presumably.

Cathy had moved to Quimby only seven months ago, and Zack Brody had been gone for approximately a year. All she knew of him as an adult were the praises sung by the townsfolk and the frequent yet affectionate complaints lodged by the Wednesday nighters.

A year should have been enough time to heal a broken heart—even five of them—but of course Heartbreak was a legend unto himself. Ordinarily, Cathy might have believed that in Zack's case time and distance had served to heighten, even exaggerate, his reputed lady-killer charms. She would have taken the women's words with not just a grain but an entire shaker of salt.

Ordinarily, she might have.

If not for her secret.

"Wait a minute, wait a minute," Allie Spangler shouted above the fray. The women quieted. "Personally, I can't believe it. Only last week—" Allie scrambled for her purse to a quartet of groans. "Okay, only a month ago, I had a postcard from Zack. He didn't mention—aha, here it is!" She pulled the item from her disorganized saddlebag of a purse, blissfully unaware that the worn card's continuing presence in her happily-married life was telling in its own way. Waving a red-rock canyon river scene at the other women, she said, "Zack's still in Idaho with his brother."

"A month ago, Allie." Julia checked the postmark. April 6th. "Make that nearly two months ago."

"So there," Gwen said. "Kelly Thompson heard from the Rickeys in Florida who are neighbors to Eve Brody's sister. Heartbreak's coming home. Soon."

"Julia?" Laurel's voice was reedy. "Is this true? What do you know?"

With the excuse that she didn't want anyone fainting in her store, Cathy was watching Laurel Barnard closely. The fellow shopkeeper's face had gone from stark white to a mottled rosy pink. There was a fine trembling about her mouth. Though Cathy's own emotions were in turmoil, she girded herself to minister first to Laurel.

Poor, poor Laurel. Heartbreak's jilted bride.

Pale, feminine, maidenly slim at twenty-eight, Laurel's air was delicate—misleadingly so, in Cathy's opinion. Then again, at hearing the news, Laurel had believably gone from merely delicate to fragile as antique porcelain. The panic in her eyes seemed very real. While Cathy had never been sure if she entirely believed Laurel's side of the cancelled wedding, she did sympathize with the woman. Being forever known as Quimby's resident jilted bride couldn't be easy.

Julia Knox capped her bottle of ink, her strong features drawn together in thought. She had been Heartbreak's long-term girlfriend—from high school through a few years of college—and yet was still the most philosophical about him. While stingy with details, she claimed their breakup had been amicable. However, she also seemed to take little serious interest in the men she'd dated in the years hence.

"I'm afraid it's true, Laurel." Julia placed her manicured hand on the other woman's sleeve. "Zack told me to take the Brody house off the market months ago."

"Months?" Gwen was outraged. "And you kept it to yourself?"

Laurel sniffled. Faith handed her a tissue.

Julia was a Realtor. *The* Realtor, insular Quimby-style. "Zack and I haven't spoken. He sent me a fax, Gwen. It didn't provide any information concrete enough to share, except that he was planning to eventually return to town."

Whatever Julia's inside information, Cathy was certain that the real estate agent wouldn't have shared inappropriate details. And definitely not with Gwen, whose heart was in the right place beneath her bluster, but whose restraint was suspect.

Upon her arrival in Quimby, Cathy had purchased her business and leased a house through Julia Knox's small but exceedingly professional agency. She'd soon seen that in business dealings, Julia was cool, efficient, responsible. Once earned as a friend, she was warm, thoughtful and unquestionably loyal. Cathy valued Julia's word above all others.

"I heard he's arriving tomorrow," Gwen said, dropping the bomb.

Faith squeaked. Laurel gasped. "Tomorrow!"

Allie's freckles stood out in stark relief; she looked like she'd swallowed a frog. "Urg," she said thickly, waving her hands.

"There's no need to get crazy over this," Julia counseled the agitated women. "Zack has every right to come back to Quimby—"

"Huh!" Gwendolyn crossed her arms over her chest, looking combative.

Laurel spoke. "I'll say this—the town's not big enough for both of us."

Cathy was startled by the seething resentment evident in Laurel's voice. Admittedly, being jilted by your catch-of-a-lifetime groom at the very altar of your dream-come-true wedding was not something a woman gets over in a week's time. A year later, though...

Cathy shrugged inwardly. Who was she to question Laurel's animosity toward Zack Brody? She, herself, had known him for only the one school year. Fifth grade, at that. And his memory had lingered for nearly two decades.

The man's charms were potent.

It stood to reason that his betrayal would be poisonous.

Evidently Julia thought so, too. When she looked at Laurel, her amber hazel eyes filled with sympathy, and something more. Perhaps a touch of exasperation? Nonetheless, she wound a comforting arm around the woman she'd known for years. "You don't have to associate with him, Laurel."

Laurel heaved a watery sigh and laid her head on Julia's shoulder. Her moment of vindictiveness had dissipated into a kind of childish helplessness that Cathy had seen her employ before. "I don't see how I can avoid it."

Gwen's eyes were avid. "You can bet he'll be showing

up everywhere, shaking hands, making amends. Heck, most of the town's already forgiven him. They still think he's the greatest thing since Oxie Shaw made the basket that beat Buxton."

"It wasn't for them to judge him in the first place." Short, auburn-haired Allie Colton Spangler was staunchly proHeartbreak. Not even the circumstances of Laurel's jilting had shaken her good opinion of the man. The Coltons and the Brodys had been neighbors; Allie had grown up with Zack. Their relationship had never been romantic—which may have been why she was the only currently married woman among them—but they had been extremely close. Even her husband accepted that Heartbreak would always own a special place in Allie's heart.

"What Zack did was wrong." Once roused, Julia's disapproval was fierce. "It may have turned out that he had a good reason, with his brother and all, but to skip town on the day of the wedding without explanation, leaving Laurel to contend with all the mess and questions—" Lips compressed, Julia shook her head in censure. "No wonder she can't forgive him."

Laurel swept aside the lustrous wave of rich chestnut hair that had fallen across her face. "Oh, I hate to remember. It was *so* humiliating...."

Faith cooed with commiseration.

Idly, Cathy drew elaborate swirls and curlicues on her practice paper. No calligraphy tonight. Since Heartbreak's actions had stuck Laurel with the role of tragic jilted heroine whether she liked it or not, the woman had chosen to play it to the hilt. There would be no quick end to the dramatic embellishments of her legendary trauma.

A temporary escape seemed advisable. Feeling guilty

about the short shrift of her sympathy for Laurel, Cathy offered to make a quick run to the Central Street Café for coffee and sweets.

When she returned ten minutes later with a tray of steaming foam cups and a box of assorted baked goods, Laurel was in better shape. Or at least sitting upright, Cathy noted as she distributed coffee, plastic spoons, and packets of sugar and cream. Progress.

"He shouldn't get away with it," Laurel said, adding a minuscule sprinkling of sugar to her coffee. Color flamed high in her cheeks; her green eyes were unnaturally bright. "I've suffered. So should he."

Cathy held her tongue. Laurel's "suffering" included the condolence gift of a fashionable dress shop by her placating parents, considerable leeway from the townsfolk and a steady string of suitors eager to restore her faith in men.

Julia agreed—with caution. "A stern scolding is in order."

Gwen snorted. "A scolding? How about a tar-and-feathering?"

Wide-eyed, Allie put down a half-eaten doughnut and wiped powdered sugar off the tips of her prominent nose and jutting chin. The unorthodox features were at odds with her bubbly personality and rounded figure. "Are we talking revenge?" Allie's eyes glinted. She may have been Zack's champion, but she was also an inveterate prankster. "Hmm. Well. Gee. Maybe one nasty turn does deserve another."

"Teach him a lesson," Gwen vowed, spraying cookie crumbs.

"Break his heart," Faith put in.

The women turned toward Faith as one, clearly struck by the idea.

The quiet secretary's gaze lowered. Her chin dropped. "Why shouldn't he know what it feels like?" she murmured into her coffee, giving them a quick glance through her colorless lashes.

As far as Cathy knew, Faith Fagan's only connection to Zack was the crush she'd been nursing ever since he'd rescued her from drowning in Mirror Lake during his suitably legendary stint as town lifeguard. The women's description of Heartbreak in swimming trunks—handsome, tanned, sporting sun-bleached highlights, a mile-wide chest and a six-pack of tight, toned abs—was so vivid that Cathy could almost see him herself when she closed her eyes and concentrated. Which she found herself doing all too often.

Gwen gave one sharp clap of her hands. "Exactly." Twice divorced, it was her contention that a formative junior-high fling with Heartbreak had ruined her for other men. Ordinary men.

Julia frowned. "Let's not be harsh."

"You know, I think Faith's hit on something." Allie was contemplative. "Now, I'm not saying I want to see Zack hurt. But it does make sense that if he were to have an inkling of how his ex-girlfriends feel, maybe he won't be quite so cavalier in his treatment of the next woman." Her long, narrow nose twitched. "And we all know there's going to be a next woman."

"With Zack," Julia said, nodding, "there always is."

"It's about time—" Gwen snapped her chocolate-chip cookie in half "—for *Heartbreak* to experience heartbreak."

"But how?" Faith asked.

"Hmm." Laurel's eyes narrowed. "All we need is a woman. A beautiful woman, obviously. Someone to attract Zack, seduce him to his begging knees, then cut him down cold. Without explanation. Leave him wondering what the hell happened." She smiled.

"That sounds kind of mean," Faith murmured.

Laurel's eyes flashed. "No meaner than what he did to me."

"I don't know..." Julia started to say, but Gwen cut her off.

"Where are we gonna find the woman?" she demanded. "Not in Quimby. Heartbreak's already scorched the playing field."

"I'm sure there are a number of younger girls who'd be more than willing," Laurel said through gritted teeth.

Julia shook her head. "A twenty-year-old won't do. Zack is attracted to more than a pretty face and a nubile body."

Laurel conceded the point. "I suppose the woman has to have a degree of substance."

"And intelligence," added Julia. "Let's throw out some names."

"Karen or Kelly?"

Gwen made a face. "Naw, he's known them forever."

"Caitlyn Dumbrowski?"

"Bleach job," Laurel sneered.

"Erica James?"

"Already hooked up with Heartbreak, like, ten years ago."

"Suzy Maki?"

"With those teeth? She should be seducing a dentist."

"Then who?"

"Sara Carlisle will be vacationing at her family's cabin next month," Julia suggested. "She's absolutely gorgeous and smart enough to have made it through law school. And a feminist, too. I bet she'd be game, for the good of the cause."

Allie waved a hand. "Nope, not Sara. Zack already went out with her—somewhere in between you and Laurel. But she was too smart to fall for his smooth moves."

"Unlike us," Gwen said, dourly eyeing a fudge bar.

"We need someone new." With a sigh, Laurel scanned the women at the table for further suggestions. Her gaze skidded to a halt when it reached Cathy's face, temporarily filled with cherry streusel. Brows arched, she glanced back at Julia. "Someone like Cathy."

Julia nodded immediately. "Yes. Zack would go for Cathy."

"Ohh—" Flushing hotly, Cathy put down the streusel and licked her sticky fingers. "Oh, no. Not me." She threw up her hands, fingertips glistening. "Don't even consider it. I'm not the type."

"You could be." Laurel studied Cathy's stark pony-tail, horn-rimmed glasses and loose, shapeless clothing. "Take off your glasses. And that awful apron."

Defensively Cathy wrapped her arms around the denim apron that bore evidence of her close working as-sociation with paint, glue, papier-mâché and clay. "No."

Laurel snatched off the glasses. "Uh-huh. See that, girls? Those are good bones. The brows desperately need tweezing, and makeup will make a world of differ-ence, but I see definite possibilities." She rose gracefully, walked around Cathy and with a tug loosened the po-nytail. Cathy's long wavy hair fell across her shoulders, such a rich shade of sable it was nearly black.

"Ahhh," the women chorused.

"Why, Cath, you're beautiful," Allie said. "I never re-alized."

"I'm not—" Cathy swallowed the denial, though it went down like a sticky lump of clay. Objectively, she knew that she was...attractive. Or could be, if she cared to make the effort. After a bit of trial and error in her younger days—a time that had included a brief audacious-babe stage and a mistaken marriage of equally short duration—she had reached the conclusion that she wasn't comfortable with the attention and perks that came with being a beautiful woman.

"I'm not the type," she insisted, shrugging Laurel's hands away from smoothing out her hair. "Please don't ask me to do this."

"You won't have to actually sleep with Heartbreak," Julia assured her. "In fact, the plan would be more effective if you don't. Getting him all worked up and then leaving him frustrated would be quite a shock to the guy's ego."

Allie chuckled. "No one's ever done *that* before."

"We'll coach you," coaxed Laurel. "For one thing—" she grasped a bunch of gauzy fabric at Cathy's midriff, pulling taut her batik Balinese blouse "—new clothes from my store would make a world of difference. Something sleek and stylish. There's a waist and hips under here...I think." She stepped back, considering.

Cathy shifted on her chair, uneasy with the assessment.

"What's your bra size? I've got a new line of lingerie that's just..." Laurel kissed her fingertips. "Heartbreak will never recover."

Cathy tightened her crossed arms. "Forget it. Nobody, least of all Zack Brody, is getting a look at my lingerie." *Or lack of it,* she thought. Jockey for Her underwear was good enough for this woman. Satin and lace, corsets and garter belts weren't her style. Or at least she was pretty sure they weren't.

"I can give you the right look," Laurel said as if Cathy

hadn't spoken. "Julia and Allie can give you insight into Heartbreak's mind. We'll put the whole thing together. All you have to do is follow directions."

"I can't," Cathy said plaintively. Good thing they had no idea how much she wanted to. "Honestly." She gestured at herself. "There's no use. I could never pull it off."

"Not even for womankind?" Allie asked.

"Or for plain old-fashioned revenge?" Gwen chimed in.

Cathy's heart clenched. "No."

"Yes," Laurel said. There was iron in her voice, which belied the hurt expression she'd assumed in begging Cathy's favor. "C'mon, Cath. You're my only hope for retribution. Imagine for one minute how terrible I felt when that—that—*smooth operator* jilted me." Laurel's eyes shifted. "Think of how delicious an appropriate payback would be."

The women murmured in agreement.

Cathy closed her eyes. "I couldn't. No..." Her denials were losing strength. But not because of Laurel's devastation or the future of womankind.

Because of Zack.

Twenty-odd years ago, she'd taken him to her tender, wounded heart. The thought of seeing him again, attracting him, seducing him, maybe even loving him—

And making him fall in love with her in return.

Cathy's eyes opened wide. Of course. That was it. She was being handed the chance of a lifetime!

The women watched her expectantly.

Cathy made a snap decision.

Disregarding both the legend behind Zack's nickname and the genesis of her own insecurities, she took a

deep breath and said with all the courage and conviction
she could muster: "All right, then. I'll do it."

The women cheered.

For my own reasons, Cathy added silently, smiling
weakly as Laurel hugged her around the shoulders.

2

ZACK BRODY hung off the side of the Eighth Street Bridge, staring down at the scalloped river. The water looked as black and hard as polished obsidian, each facet glistening coldly in the light from a crescent moon.

The drop was harrowing.

He hesitated, considering, where once he'd have leapt without fear.

This early in the summer, the water would be cold. Shockingly cold.

Deep. Dark. An oblivion.

His fingertips scraped over rough stone. Bare feet shifted on a narrow ledge of rock, sending a pebble toward the water. Too small for him to hear its splash.

Adam, he thought, his gaze rising to the glowing slice of moon. *Laurel*.

Suddenly Zack propelled himself off the old stone bridge, his body arching as it sailed through the dark night. For one frozen-snapshot instant, he saw only the blue evening sky, dotted with stars. Then dense treetops, the blur of house lights. A slab of black water seemed to rush up to meet him.

He sliced into it like a blade, his form lacking from his swim team days, but adequate nonetheless. Darkness swirled all around, silvered with tiny bubbles. The harsh cold bit into him, reaching the marrow of his bones, the shock of it driving every thought from his head.

He hung suspended in the depths for one instant, then shot upward, lungs bursting, blood pumping. *Home*, he thought, breaking the surface, gulping air through an open mouth. *Home at last.*

And this time he was glad of it.

He began to swim, leaving the keys in his unlocked Jag without a second thought. He'd been gone not quite a year; Quimby wouldn't have changed. It never had before. This was something he liked about his hometown. Excitement and challenge he'd found elsewhere, with his job as an architect at a cutting-edge Chicago firm. Quimby was for friends, family, bedrock values and lazy Sunday afternoons. Now that he was back, he and Laurel would establish a mutually workable truce. The town, though small, was still big enough for both of them. Even if he decided to stay for good.

He swam briskly, his muscles loosening even though the river was colder than he'd expected. Vastly unlike the heated pool at Adam's gym in Twin Falls where they'd swum five days out of seven for many months. That had been like being dunked in a bucket of warm soup. This was better.

It had jolted him back to life.

Zack put his head down and plowed through the water, leaving only a narrow furrow of wake.

The memories churning inside him were more disruptive. On the eve of his wedding to Laurel Barnard, a serious car accident had put his estranged brother in the hospital and then in a wheelchair, fighting to regain the ability to walk. Despite the complications of the situation, perhaps *because* of them, Zack's first obligation had been to Adam. Each day, each month of therapy had strengthened his younger brother's body and eased

Zack's guilt, until, finally, both of them were healed. Both of them forgiven.

Now to mend other broken fences. Zack lifted his head from the water, checking his progress. He'd swum past the bend. The Brody house was another seventy yards away, though only the peak of the roof and an expanse of dark shingles were visible amongst the lacy, draped foliage of the weeping willows lining the riverbank.

Already the homey, comforting tranquility of Quimby was sinking into Zack's pores. The still of the night was broken only by a smattering of porch lights, the blare of a television set near an open window, the shush-swish of the water as he cut through it. A lone bird called from one of the trees. Loop-loop-de-loop.

One foot touched bottom. The other. Cold mud sucked at his ankles. He crashed through the reeds, rising from the water with the heavy denim of his jeans plastered to his thighs.

He splashed noisily as he charged out of the river, expelling the cold from his lungs with a bullish snort followed by an exuberant shout. After climbing the slippery bank, he stopped near the white iron lawn furniture to press water out of his jeans in a gush, and realized his mistake. His wallet and all of his keys were in the car, parked at the bridge. He'd have to walk back there, shirtless, barefoot, dripping wet.

He laughed out loud, his skin already shuddering into goose bumps. A fine welcome home.

But first the house.

Thank God it hadn't sold during the months when he'd thought he'd never care to return to Quimby. The old place was comfortably the same. A two-story white frame structure, simple and pleasing in proportion, encircled by an open porch whose roof was supported by gracefully turned columns.

He left a wet trail through the freshly mown grass as he strode up the lawn to the low brick patio that extended the outdoor living space. Though there were none of his mother's usual pots of flowers and herbs, the lilacs were still in bloom, drooping with purple cones of flowers that had begun to turn brown. The massive rhododendron bush that had consumed the narrow span of land between the Brody house and the Colton's modest two-story cottage next door was bursting with pink buds.

He surveyed the lawn. No evidence of debris, weeds, scattered leaves or twigs. Julia had been as efficient as ever with the maintenance; no doubt she'd hired Reggie Lee Marvin, the town's resident jack-of-all-trades, to do the yard work.

Zack crossed the patio, leaving more wet footprints on the redbrick. While his heart was warmed by his return home, the rest of him was slowly turning to ice. Shivering, he mounted the porch steps to check the back door. Locked, of course. Even in Quimby, Julia would not leave a house in her care unlocked.

As he walked around the porch, his gaze rose to the roof. The second-story bedroom windows might be open. Adam had been an expert at shinnying up the columns after a curfew-breaking night of escapades. Zack, the good son, had rarely found the need.

An echo of Adam's boyish taunt seemed to float on the night air. *Anything you can do, I can do better....*

Zack's features tightened. He deliberately tamped down the memory. The brothers' good-natured rivalry had grown serious upon Laurel Barnard's involvement. Tragically, as it had turned out.

If only he'd known. If only their confrontation had been straight and cool instead of a clash of mistaken pride and misleading accusations.

As for Laurel...

Her intentions remained indecipherable.

A breeze fingered through the foliage, carrying a faint whiff of the lilac's sweet perfume. The smell brought up a sickening memory—the night he'd proposed to Laurel. Zack leaned against the smooth white column, his stomach lurching.

What the hell? he asked himself, swallowing the dry coppery taste in his mouth. His return to Quimby wasn't supposed to go like this. Granted, he hadn't expected the usual favorite-son-arriving-in-a-blaze-of-glory welcome. But a year had passed. By now, the misunderstandings—and outright lies—that had led to the ditched wedding were all water under the bridge, for lack of a better phrase. The brothers had forgiven each other, and Zack held no grudge against Laurel. Whatever her motive, she'd been desperate. And pregnant.

Perhaps.

He raked his hands through his wet hair, glancing up when a light went on next door. Were the Coltons home? They might still have his spare key. Allie, who lived outside of town with her own family now, had said her parents were loving California so much they'd instructed her to pack up their parkas and snow boots and take them to Goodwill. But that had been a while back.

Zack angled his head. A light was on in the master bedroom, painting the windowpanes a buttery gold through a pair of sheer curtains. Tenants, maybe.

A woman in a towel and nothing else walked past the lit window. An instantaneous heat blowtorched his groin.

Because the towel was on her head.

Leaving the rest of her...

Naked.

"Sweet Mary," said Zack's lips, all on their own.

The rest of him was pleading. *Please come back.*

He stared, no longer feeling the dampness or the cold. Oxygen was short in his lungs. He stood tall, crossing his arms on top of his head, sucking in the night air without noticing the lilac's lingering scent.

His chest expanded.

His gaze fixed on the partly raised window.

Imagine that. The Coltons' new tenant was either completely uninhibited or had lived in the house long enough to take the lack of neighbors for granted. Possibly she didn't realize how clearly one could see through the flimsy curtains she'd drawn across the window. Particularly with the light on.

If that were the case, he should look away.

He meant to. Until she came back. And sat, presumably at the foot of the bed, although he couldn't quite tell from his ground-level position.

After a moment of fiddling, she held out one arm and luxuriously stroked the opposite palm across it. Lotion, he thought, catching the glisten of pearly moisture on pale skin. Her palms rubbed together. Eyes closed, she threw back her turbanned head. Arched her throat. Slick fingers slithered across her exposed neck and delicate collarbone in a languid caress.

One palm slid to her nape. Her head lolled, turning her face toward the window. The curtains fluttered, giving Zack a glimpse of starkly lit detail. She was beautiful. Creamy skin, cheeks tinged with a pink warmth from the bath. Full, pursed lips. Thick lashes, dark brows, drawn like black ink against the cameo of her face.

Zack blinked. What was he doing—concentrating on her face? Sheesh. If he was going to be crude, might as well do it right.

His gaze lowered incrementally, in sync with her hands. She rubbed lotion over her upper chest, then slid both hands lower, cupping her left breast, lifting it slightly. His mouth watered, imagining the weight of it in his own palm, the flavor of it on his tongue. The breast was small, but full and round, centered by a pale brown areola.

The curtains billowed, giving him a clearer look. Hands clenching, eyes narrowing, he concentrated his vision down to a laser point as the woman's nipple drew into a small tight bead.

Desire raced his pulse. She was incredible. A fantasy sprung to life.

The breeze died, dropping the sheer veil of fabric into place. Still, he couldn't have looked away even if he'd wanted to. The woman was massaging a sheen of lotion into her breast, carelessly grazing her nails over the knotted nipple. He ached to give it more attention. Only when she reached again for the lotion, blocking his intimate view, did he remember where he was and what he was doing.

Ogling. Leering.

And in Quimby, too. Favored son or not, the chief of police would slam Zack into a jail cell for committing such a crime against common decency. Regardless of the rest of the world, the law-abiding local citizenry still claimed to believe in modesty and morality.

Zack backed toward the deep shadows beneath the porch. Slowly. Even though the woman was rubbing lotion into her other breast with a circular motion that made his blood run hot from his scalp all the way down to the numbed soles of his bare feet.

She reached forward, folding a leg up to her chest. The motion made the coiled towel tumble from her head, releasing a thick skein of wet dark hair. With a sound of dismay, she tossed back her head—and froze. Her eyes widened, their stricken gaze glued to the fluttering curtain.

Zack eased toward the shadows.

With the towel bunched against her bare breasts, the woman flew to the window and peered out. Her mouth was open. She seemed to be breathing hard, her face aflame beneath the sheaf of dark hair. He took another big step backward, trusting the overhang of the porch roof that now blocked his view would deny hers as well.

After a long tense moment and one last breathy exclamation, he heard the sash slam and the clatter of blinds descending with unseemly speed. Had she spotted him?

The probability made him smile.

Mmm. Turned out his early, unexpected homecoming had its pluses after all.

CATHY'S VOICE shook as she spoke into the cordless phone. "What does Zack Brody look like?"

"You've seen photos," said Julia Knox, off-handedly. Confused that her embarrassment was sprinkled with what seemed a lot like titillation, Cathy hadn't explained why she was asking.

"I've seen Laurel's engagement photo. The one she uses as a pincushion." Cathy squinted as she parted the slatted blinds. The Brody house next door was dark and silent; perhaps she'd been mistaken. Which could be worse. If the peeper wasn't Zack Brody, then who...? Did she want the frying pan or the fire?

No choice. "What does he look like without a gazillion pins sticking out of his face?"

Julia chuckled. "Oh, he's a handsome sonovagun."

Cathy gritted her teeth. "Well, gosh, I know *that*."

Zack Brody's looks were as legendary as the rest of him. There were those who said he should have followed Eunice LaSalle to Hollywood; the younger generation was more likely to suggest a male modeling career in New York. His photographs were prominent in several locations throughout Quimby, including athletic team pictures in the trophy cases at the high school and an award-winning senior photo on permanent display at the local photography studio. Good old Heartbreak was even in evidence at city hall. When Cathy had gone to get her business license, there was a black-and-white Zack smiling out at her, snapped in the act of receiving a commendation from the mayor for his lifesaving rescue of Faith Fagan at Mirror Lake. Naturally, she'd studied the shot. Zack's charisma had shone even in a still photograph. He was handsome, clean-cut, very Kennedy-esque in the best of ways. But, at twenty, still a boy.

Cathy said as much to Julia, wanting to know what he might look like now...when he was stripped to the waist, every bared muscle wet and glistening. Without her glasses, she hadn't gotten a clear look at his face. But the body had left a lasting impression.

"Ah, there you go." Julia sounded far too cheerful. "Zack only gets better looking as he ages. He's an adult now, you see, not just an exceptionally handsome young man. His masculine pulchritude's at full power."

You bet. Cathy tried to transfer the pin-pricked face of

Laurel's fiancé onto the virile body she'd glimpsed in the shadows beneath the Brody's porch.

She sank onto the bed, her joints soft as pudding. "I don't think I can do this."

Julia understood at once. "Nonsense. It's going to be such fun. We won't let it go too far."

Cathy thought of her unwitting exposure at the open window and gave a dry laugh that turned into a cough. By all appearances, she was *way* past too far.

"Er, Julia...when exactly is Zack due to return?"

"Sometime tomorrow."

"You're sure?"

"He's pretty reliable."

"Except when it comes to weddings."

"Mmm, there is that."

Cathy sighed. "Julia? Do you believe Laurel's side of the story?"

"There's been no evidence to the contrary."

"But from what you've said, it sounds like Zack hasn't been in contact since he left. Other than to ask you to look after the house."

"His silence is awfully suspicious."

Cathy tugged up her towel, her own silence skeptical.

"Shoot," said Julia, "we wouldn't even have learned about his brother's accident if it weren't for Gwen's persistent nosiness. Zack knows how much we all care for Adam. We'd've liked to have known how he was doing."

"Well, see—that's what I mean." Cathy wondered why she was defending a man called Heartbreak. Especially when the odds were that she'd end up his next victim. "I don't blame Laurel for being put out, but considering that he cancelled because of a family emergency..."

"If he'd stopped to explain, sure, we'd all have understood." Julia's tone grew mulish. "But he didn't. He left poor Laurel stranded at the church in a five-thousand-dollar designer wedding gown. There were six bridesmaids. Seventy-five guests. Seventy-five plates of salmon in mint sauce. It was a frigging fiasco."

"I suppose so."

"All part of Heartbreak's pattern."

Cathy hesitated. "He's that bad?"

"How shall I put it?" Julia's laugh was contemplative. Maybe even nostalgic. "Aw, Cath. You won't fully understand until you meet him, but the best I can explain is that Zack is so darn good he's bad."

"So *good?*"

"The best. The ultimate smooth operator. Every woman he dates thinks she's died and gone to heaven. Next to the usual mouth-breathing social cretins that pass for eligible bachelors in Quimby, Zack's a sweet-talking miracle. No girl can resist. And, wow, believe me, it's great while it lasts."

"But?"

"But then the dream ends," Julia said evenly. "One day, one way or another, you wake up and realize Zack's moved on to the next woman just when you were getting ready to order the monogrammed towels. And then you don't even get the pleasure of hating him because he's so incredibly charming even when he's dumping you."

Cathy blinked at the phone. "I'd be devastated."

"Yup." Julia sounded anything but. "And that's why we call him Heartbreak."

"Yet you still like him," Cathy said. "I can tell. All of you *adore* him."

"That's Heartbreak's greatest skill. He's the only man

on earth who's on friendly terms with all of his former girlfriends. As good as he is at romance—and he's excellent—he's the world's best breaker-upper.''

It was some comfort, Cathy decided. If she did get with the plan and play up to Zack, the worst that could happen would be that he'd let her down easy. Which wouldn't be so bad. Really. She'd have plenty of company, and the consolation that at least she'd made the attempt. Maybe she'd be spoiled for other men, as Gwen said, but that would be nothing new.

There had to be a loophole she was missing. ''You're saying Laurel doesn't count?''

''Oh, Laurel,'' Julia scoffed. ''Sure, she's out for revenge. Her pride was hurt pretty spectacularly. But if Zack so much as crooked a finger at her, she'd go running into his arms, I guarantee it. Even if it was just for the thrill of planning another fancy wedding. Wouldn't surprise me a bit if she's saved the dress for a second go-round.''

Cathy returned to the window and peeked out again. ''You think?''

This time, Julia's laugh was faintly bittersweet. ''Laurel's been after Zack for as long as I can remember. And she's determined to make a 'good' marriage. Not just anyone will do.''

Still no sign of occupancy next door. ''I've never understood why it wasn't you he was marrying,'' Cathy ventured. Julia was intelligent, personable, polished; she seemed like Zack Brody's perfect mate. More than any of the other women.

Including myself, Cathy admitted.

''Oh, well, what can I say?'' There was a shrug in the Realtor's voice. ''Zack and I had split way before Laurel finally got her shot.''

"Sounds as though you took it well."

Julia's pause was short. "We'd run our course."

"No hard feelings, huh?" But not a little regret, Cathy surmised.

"Having your heart broken by Zack Brody is a singular experience."

Cathy made herself laugh. "One you want me to share?"

"Ah, but we're not sending you in unprepared. This time will be different, I promise. It's not *your* heart at risk."

"Gosh, I sure hope so." Cathy's attempt at levity rang hollow. She shivered instead, her arms clamping the towel around her torso.

"Just remember," Julia said, "Heartbreak's comeuppance is long overdue."

Which was not what Cathy intended, but Julia wouldn't welcome the confession. Besides, Cathy was doubtful about whether she'd be capable of the duplicity necessary when it came to the crunch, let alone the too-farfetched-to-contemplate seduction aspect of the whole business.

Unless it really had been Zack watching her from the porch next door. If so, she'd mistakenly gotten off to the best—make that *breast*—start imaginable.

Hah. Maybe he hadn't gotten a very good look through the curtains, at such an angle.

Then again, maybe he had.

She leaned against the wall, weighing her reaction to the possibility that he'd seen everything. Both her instant embarrassment and the subsequent attack of nerves were what she'd expected. More surprising was the exquisite seeping warmth caused by the thought of continuing the game. *Imagine seducing Zack*, she thought, and her lips parted in anticipation. She expelled a soft breath. With her new friends' help, she might even be able to do it successfully.

"Now, Cath," Julia said, bringing her back to the conversation. "Please stop worrying. You'll do splendidly."

"But I can't—I'm not—I have no...va-va-voom," she said, having unexpectedly caught sight of herself in between the scarves she'd draped around the cheval mirror. "It's plain to see." Disregarding the limpid look in her eyes, she dragged her fingers through her tangled hair, adjusted the drooping towel. "What you want is someone with more, uh, obvious enticements."

Julia tsk-tsked. "Not for Zack."

"He's a guy, isn't he?"

"But a guy with discerning tastes."

He almost married Laurel, Cathy realized. How discerning could he be?

Oh, that wasn't fair. Laurel Barnard was certainly lovely. And often friendly, if slightly reserved. She managed her dress shop with skill and pride. Her personality was, at times, pleasant. She was just...a tad weak in the character department.

And Cathy set great store by character.

She made a face at her reflection. Pot calling the kettle black. For goodness sake, she was about to embark on a superficial seduction ploy of epic proportions! She, the woman who ranked appearance below "showers daily" and "knows how to read" among the qualities she looked for in the opposite sex.

It won't be superficial if it's about love, whispered the hopeless romantic part of her that had yearned after Zack since fifth grade.

And, woo, girl, you sure could use the help, countered the self-doubting voice that she'd never quite been able to vanquish. The cruelty she'd once endured as a homely, chubby, social outcast had blighted her confidence. Even to this day, though rationally she understood that she'd always been a worthy person. School yard taunts shouldn't—didn't—matter.

Way back when, the friendship of a spirited, confident ten-year-old boy named Zack Brody had been the only kindness she'd known. He was the one new schoolmate who'd seen the girl she was inside, not out. Long after she'd moved away and grown up and become "beautiful," she'd remembered Zack for that.

And she'd remembered the little town of Quimby.

Cathy turned away from the mirror. Toward the window. Toward Zack.

"We'll coach you every step of the way," Julia was saying reassuringly into her ear when a light blinked on next door.

The bottom dropped out of Cathy's stomach. Oh, my.

There was a racy black sports car parked in the driveway of the Brody house. Inside, another light came on.

Cathy's fingers clenched, putting creases into the miniblinds. She closed her eyes. Zack. Zack Brody.

Heartbreak was home.

And—

Oh. My. Stars.

He'd *seen* her.

3

THE NEXT DAY, Cathy worked at Scarborough Faire alone all morning. Its herbal-scented atmosphere soothed her fitfulness. Amongst the shop's cornucopia of gnarled branches and vines, sheaves of dried flowers, weathered barn-board shelving, old jelly cupboards and pie safes stocked with ribbons and wrapping papers, stationery, pen nibs and bottles of ink, she was as at home and confident as never before in her life. Peace had its price in this instance; few customers stopped in. Distracted from issues of commerce, she did not particularly care.

Quite naturally, Cathy was occupied with thoughts of Zack Brody. Worriedly, at first, but after a few hours in the shop, she began to see things from a different perspective. A buoyant, emboldened one.

And why not? She was attractive enough. She was intelligent. She was capable.

Upon realizing how dissatisfied she'd become with her humdrum life as an accounts supervisor for a small advertising firm in Virginia Beach, she'd single-handedly researched, plotted and executed a successful escape. She'd ditched the job, cashed out her savings and moved cross-country to turn Kay's Krafts into the storybook arts and gift shop she'd long dreamed of.

Such drastic change took courage. Ergo, she'd already proved that she could handle anything.

Even, perhaps, the legendary Heartbreak.

Humming beneath her breath, Cathy rummaged through an old sea chest of fabric remnants. Zack had nearly caught her that morning when she'd scurried from the house to her car, wearing dark glasses and a scarf knotted over her hair like a celebrity dodging the paparazzi.

He'd stepped onto his porch and shouted a neigh-borly hello; she'd been reversing out of the driveway and had pretended not to notice. All she'd seen was a quick glimpse of him in her rearview mirror. Upraised hand, fading smile. Thick brown hair. Lots of shoulder.

Imminent Heartbreak.

Cathy pulled out a piece of gingham, then discarded it. Whether or not anything developed between her and Zack, she was willing to be a martyr for the cause.

Unfolding a length of dotted swiss, she thought of his engaging smile, the light in his eyes. Her stomach did a slow roll of sensuous proportions. Yum. There were worse fates.

At one o'clock, Kay Estress arrived for the shift she put in four days a week. As the store's previous propri-etor, Kay had agreed to stay on part-time during the changeover of ownership. Seven months later, though appreciative of the practical advice Kay freely—and fre-quently—offered, Cathy was ready for the arrangement to end. She hadn't yet figured out how to ease Kay out the door in a properly respectful manner.

The tall, raw-boned woman gave the new baby-bootie-and-receiving-blanket display a once-over. Cathy had gone a little wild with the dotted swiss and trailing yellow ribbons.

Kay, whose style was relentlessly straightforward, even militant, sniffed. "Cute," she conceded, her dark brows rising to meet the fluff of silvery-white bangs that were the only soft thing about her. "But it doesn't pay to overstock on these type of knitting patterns. The profit margin is minimal."

Cathy took off her apron, wadded it up and stowed it on one of the shelves beneath the checkout counter. "A person who buys the patterns will need needles, ribbon and two kinds of yarn," she pointed out. "We—*I'll* see a decent return."

Kay shrugged her wide, bony shoulders. "It's your funeral." She slipped a pristine apron over the neat silver cap of her hair, straightening her starched collar with a tug. *Her* displays had been practical, not imaginative. *Her* shelves had been stocked on schedule, not on whim.

Cathy smiled at Kay. Nicely. She understood that it was difficult for the older woman to adjust to a more creative way of doing things. Having grown up under the watch of Admiral Wallace Winston Bell, Cathy had plenty of experience dealing with rigidity. Her father was career Navy—he'd run the proverbial tight ship. His awkward, bookish, imaginative daughter had baffled him to no end. He'd never completely succeeded in shaping her up, which was perhaps the one failure in his illustrious career.

"I'll be gone for at least an hour," Cathy said, tightening at the thought of her impending makeover. "Maybe two."

Kay took out a bottle of Zap, her favorite spray cleaner. "No problem."

Cathy waved from the door. "There haven't been many customers, so you should do fine alone. I'll be next door at Laurel's if you need me."

Kay doffed the bottle as Cathy departed. Looking back, she saw that her employee had yanked the apron out from beneath the counter and was whipping it into a tidy package like a color guard folding a flag. A woman after her father's heart. Banish the thought.

Outside, the June sunshine was glorious; it made the pavement shine and the parking meters sparkle. Quimby was as quaint as Cathy had remembered from her yearlong stay as a child. Beneath mature sugar maples and grand old elms, the residential streets were cozy with modest Queen Anne cottages, Craftsman bungalows and wood-frame houses with wide front porches. The downtown business district thrived on what passed for bustle in the small town. Cathy did not regret her move, even though it had meant leaving several good friends and her one dominant family member behind.

Luckily, her second sojourn in Quimby had thus far not been as socially inept as the first, when she'd been sent to stay with her grandparents while the Admiral was at sea. She'd made plenty of friends this time around, and even gone out on a few pleasant dates. In fact, the residents were so friendly she rarely stepped outside of her little shop without being greeted by several of them.

"Hallo, Mrs. Timmerman," said Reggie Lee Marvin, his face completely guileless beneath the bill of a grimy, faded gimme cap. The handyman parked his three-wheeled bike at the curb. A toolbox, spade, rake and other assorted supplies were strapped to the basket in the back.

"Hey, Reggie Lee. Isn't it a beautiful day?"

"Sure is, Mrs. Timmerman."

"Going to lunch?" Cathy had given up trying to get Reggie Lee to call her Cathy, or even Ms. or Miss. She'd never felt much like a Mrs. Her marriage to Chad Timmerman, handsome hunk but faithless husband, had lasted all of two years, including the divorce process.

Reggie Lee nodded, his full cheeks turning ruddy. Cathy suspected he had a bit of a crush on her, as was also the case with Laurel, Julia and perhaps even Faith. She'd seen Reggie Lee watching Faith with an absorbed expression.

The handyman was far too shy to be overt toward the opposite sex. He ducked his head when addressing her, avoiding eye contact. "You coming to the café, Mrs. Timmerman?"

Cathy stepped under a white canvas awning and opened the door to Laurel's store, Couturier, which was as high style as Quimby got. "Not today, Reggie Lee. But I'll see you around."

"Okey-dokey."

Allie was tugging on Cathy's arm before she'd even made it over the threshold into the elegant store. "Come on, chickie. We've been waiting for you. There's lots and lots to do."

"Well, gee, thanks," Cathy said with dry amusement.

Allie chuckled. "Cripes, Cath. You know what I mean."

"Sure. I know." She pressed a hand to her tie-dyed head scarf, feeling at odds with Couturier's many mirrored surfaces and its refined decor of monochromatic pewter accented by touches of glossy black. "I'm... ready." The makeover was dreaded, but necessary. Part of her even *wanted* it. For Zack.

"Ewww." Laurel came out of the back room with puckered lips and an armful of garments. "You must take that rag off your head, Cathy. It's so very sixties. And the blouse...how ethnic." She shuddered. "That won't do."

Cathy dragged off the scarf and shook out her hair. "What's wrong with ethnic?" Her closet was filled with imported clothing. The pieces she'd collected were inexpensive, colorful, unique and easy to wear. No binding straps, formfitting skirts or low-cut necklines to worry about.

"Since this is a makeover, I'll be straight with you." Laurel's smile made a token apology. "First of all, you couldn't seduce a marine fresh off the ship in *that* gunnysack."

Cathy tucked her hands into the roomy pockets of the plain dress and turned to examine it in a triple mirror. The ticking pinafore was both comfortable and suitable for her work; she'd paired it with a red cotton embroidered blouse from Mexico. It looked okay to her. But Laurel knew fashion, and she certainly knew what attracted men.

"This one will bring out the blue in your eyes." Laurel held up a periwinkle slip dress. It dangled from a hanger on skinny straps, shimmering in the artfully arranged lights that beamed from brushed steel fixtures overhead, spilling in subtle pools here and there on the plush gray carpeting.

Cathy gulped. "But there's nothing to that dress."

Laurel's lips curved. "Exactly."

Allie was looking at Cathy's chunky sandals. "You'll need heels."

"I can't walk in heels."

"Oh, great." Laurel rolled her eyes an instant before she turned her face aside.

"I know." Ignoring her scraped pride, Cathy took off her glasses and squinted. The details of her reflection were becomingly blurred. "I'm a major project." As much as the prospect of lipstick and heels and daring hemlines dismayed her, she didn't ask the women to quit. A psychologically interesting development. Perhaps now that she'd accomplished a career switch, she was ready to change her appearance as well...?

"Add contacts to the to-do list," Laurel said.

"I have contacts. They make my eyes itch and water."

"You can do this, Cathy." Allie was encouraging while she searched her purse for the list they'd started at the calligraphy class. "*We* can do this."

Julia and Faith arrived, both on their lunch hour. Gwen was peeved that she couldn't get free from her job at the post office and was missing all the makeover fun.

Faith seated herself on an unobtrusive brushed aluminum chair and opened her neat little brown-bag lunch. Julia flipped through the garments, munching on a juicy apple, ignoring Laurel's murmurs and fluttering hands.

"Whew. Hot tamale." Broodingly, Julia admired a slinky, strapless dress in a deep shade of brick-red. When her gaze turned toward Cathy, she frowned. "You know, it occurs to me..." She glanced at the other women. "Sure, we can glam Cathy up like a living doll, but how will that make her different from every other girl Zack has already had?"

Julia pitched the apple core and wiped her hands on the piece of silver wrapping tissue Laurel hastily provided. "I'm thinking this seduction has to be as emotional as it is physical."

Laurel narrowed her eyes. "And how does one accomplish that?"

"With a provocative brain tease, not slam-bang, bam-between-the-eyes lust."

Apprehension nibbled at Cathy's composure. Each

glimpse of Zack, in photographs or in person, had been like a kick in the gut. Was that lust or was that more?

"Nothing too obvious," Julia continued. "Heartbreak shouldn't know he's being played."

Cathy winced over the previous evening. Prancing around naked definitely fit under the "obvious" category.

"These clothes *are* subtle," Laurel said, miffed. "I'm not offering peekaboo bras and crotchless panties."

"Yes, of course. But clothes are beside the point." Julia advanced on Cathy, watching as her face colored with discomfiture. "Oh, Cath. You're so innocent. We need to play up that sexy, who-me? quality of yours."

Cathy caught at her lower lip. "I didn't know I had one."

"Exactly." Julia took her by the shoulders and turned her toward the mirror. "You've been hiding your light under the proverbial bushel up to now. Let yourself shine. Use your smarts, your smile. The genuine *you* will get Zack's attention, not the fancy frills. All we need to do is set the proper stage."

Julia's words worked a transformation on Cathy. She drew a deep breath, lifted her chin. She was strong, she reminded herself. She was smart. As for sexy...well, she could always fake that.

Because she was woman. Incomparable, undeniable, phenomenal woman.

You can do this, she told her reflection, momentarily entranced by the lift of her amused smile, the slant of her chin. The gleam in her squinting eyes. *Zack's worth the effort. And the potential humiliation.*

"Yes." Julia gave her a squeeze. "Go for it."

Faith goggled, a bitten tuna sandwich suspended halfway to her mouth.

Allie said, "Wow," and dove her head into her purse.

"But remember, this is only a make-believe seduction," warned Laurel, her airy tone edged in ice. She held up a pair of tweezers like forceps. "The purpose is to give Heartbreak a taste of his own medicine."

"Of course," Cathy murmured, scarcely listening.

Though Julia lifted a discerning brow, she didn't say a word.

"SO WHAT'S WITH my new neighbor?" Zack said, applying his elbow to Fred Spangler's gut when the man attempted a rush toward the basketball. Zack dribbled around his old college friend, made a feint that put Fred further off balance, then pulled up and sent the ball arching toward the basket.

Swish.

Fred staggered off the court, red-faced and dripping with sweat. "You win. Again. Man, Zack." He collapsed onto a bench. "Thought you said you'd gone soft in Idaho."

"Not soft enough." Zack grabbed the spinning ball off the cement court and beamed it toward Fred's bulging midsection. "Allie's turned into a good cook?"

Fred caught the ball and shot it back as hard as he could. "She's terrible."

The ball slammed into Zack's waiting hands. He laughed, glad to be home, among friends with a shared history. "Yeah. I remember her Home Ec experiments. Chicken-fried salmon. Salsa-flavored taffy. Snow pea flambé."

"Since the kids came, Allie's given up on cooking. The munchkins get PB&Js. The adults get Chinese take-out three times a week. She even lets me order in pizza at midnight." Fred yanked off his sweatband, releasing a floppy halo of golden curls. "It's great. Just like our fraternity days. Except with a woman at hand there's also regular sex."

"Married sex."

"Way better than college sex, bud."

"Maybe for you."

"Yeah, well, we can't all be the campus heartthrob."

Zack shrugged. "I never applied for the job."

"I know, man, I know. The coeds just handed it to ya." Fred cackled. "It's a nasty job..."

"But someone's got to do it," Zack finished, somewhat sheepishly. He'd never intended to become known as a ladies' man. He'd just always done what he'd been brought up to do. Which was the right thing. The polite thing. The considerate, generous, honorable thing.

Women seemed to appreciate it.

He palmed the basketball and held it threateningly over Fred's blond head. "Say, Shirley T, you're never gonna rev up enough to beat me subsisting on take-out food. Try tofu instead."

Fred sneered at the old nickname, braced himself for a ball bouncing off his skull, and asked mildly, "You eat health food?"

Zack set the ball on the bench. He swiped his damp forehead with the ragged hem of his T-shirt. The light breeze cooled the hot skin of his abdomen. "It's not so bad."

"Yeah, sure. You just go for the nature girls. Long hair. No bras. Equal opportunity *Kama Sutra*." Fred squinted into the sunshine. "Got a recipe?"

"For Allie?" In Allie's hands, tofu would take on terrifying configurations. Maybe Fred was referring to one of the more complicated positions from the dog-eared copy of the *Kama Sutra* they'd studied in college, some of which *ought* to come with a recipe. And scorecard.

"Naw," Fred said. "For me. One of us has got to learn how to cook healthy pretty damn soon. The sex won't be much good if I can't see past my gut."

"Exercise," said Zack. "Swimming. Low-impact aerobics." He slanted a smile at Fred. "Good for the stamina. I'm sure Allie'd appreciate it."

"Don't you worry. Allie's a tiger in the sack. Got enough stamina for both of us."

"Hey, that's my childhood pal you're talking sleaze about." Zack scooped up the ball, bounced it a few times, went up on the balls of his feet and lined up another perfect shot.

Swish.

Fred groaned. "Show-off."

Zack let the ball roll away along the cracked cement. They'd chosen to play one-on-one at the old Riverpark courts instead of the busy set of courts at the youth center. Zack was still unsure of his reception. The Barnards had a lot of friends around town and he hadn't felt like running into their public disapproval quite yet.

He walked to the bench and sat, then flexed his hands and laid them on his thighs. "So."

Fred lifted an arm and took a sniff. "Man. I stink like a goat. Gotta go home and take a shower before I head back to the car lot."

"What about the neighbor?" Zack prodded.

"Eh. Allie knows her. But she's not your type." Fred rested his head against the chain-link fence. He made quotation marks in the air, his tenor rising and falling like a graph. "She's *creative.* Which translates to *sensitive* and *temperamental* in my book. *High maintenance.* She presides over a coven of crafty women at her store on Central Street."

"And her name?" Zack thought of the woman, splendidly nude, bathed in golden light, a visual poem of languid female grace. She'd been natural, yet seductive. Enchanting. Even today, he was feeling kind of strung out, empty and restless, hungry for another sight of her.

"Cathy Timmerman," Fred said with a grunt. "New in town."

"Boyfriend?"

"How would I know?"

"Allie."

Fred scratched his head. "Yeah, like I listen when she talks."

In college, he'd fallen hard and fast for Allie the first time she'd visited Zack. Within a day, Fred had shaved off his incipient goatee, torn down his Cindy Crawford posters and started dogging Allie like a Springer Spaniel. At the moment, Zack was too lazily distracted to point that out.

"Man, your radar must be off," Fred complained. "Trust me, Zack. You don't want this one—she wears baggy clothes, Birkenstocks and Mr. Magoo glasses. She's not in your league." Absently, he stroked his belly. "Hell, I don't think her type even has a league."

"Outside of softball, neither do I." Were they talking about the same woman? They had to be. Instead of being put off, Zack felt...privileged. As if Cathy Timmerman's beauty was his alone.

"Yeah, sure," scoffed Fred. "Like Laurel Barnard isn't in a class by herself. Talk about high maintenance!"

Laurel. Zack gritted his teeth until his jaw bulged.

"Yup." Fred nudged his pal in the ribs. "Laurel. She's still mad at you."

"I assumed as much."

"I heard she said that if you ever showed your face in town again, she was gonna sic her daddy on you. Planned to sue you big time—public humiliation, alienation of affection, something like that. She's out to recoup the cost of the, uh, wedding." Fred glanced sidelong at Zack. "I'd be worried if I was you. Laurel's got a hidden nasty streak."

Not entirely hidden. "Hmm. Guess I'll start rounding up character witnesses."

Fred leaned forward and put his elbows on his knees. "Steer clear, is all I'm saying."

"What about Julia? Does she hate me, too?"

"With her, who knows? Jule doesn't run off at the mouth like the rest of 'em."

Zack expelled a huge breath.

Fred's shoulders hunched. "Gotta be strange for you, being the whipping boy instead of the hero."

"The whipping boy?"

"Women take weddings mighty seriously. And vanishing grooms—" He whistled, slowly wagging his head from side to side.

In Zack's note to Laurel, he'd offered to pay for half of the cost of the cancelled wedding; he'd even provided Adam's temporary address. She'd never responded. A matter of hurt pride, he'd assumed, and possibly even remorse for her part in the fiasco.

He shoved the matter to the back of his mind, leaving it for a personal confrontation with Laurel that was coming as surely as the next Quimby garage sale. "Stuff that," he told Fred. "I'd rather talk about my new neighbor."

"Why her? You can't be that hard up."

"What do you mean? She's..." Zack waved his hands in the air.

Fred scratched his scalp vigorously, making the yellow mop of hair slide back and forth. "We are talking about Cathy Timmerman, the woman who's renting Allie's family's house?"

"None other." Zack's face felt warm, and not because of the sun. There had to be a dopey look on it, too, judging by his friend's baffled expression.

"This is weird," said Fred.

"Very."

"Something's not right."

Oh, but it is, Zack thought. *Very right.*

He'd bet what was left of his good reputation on it.

ZACK TOOK his time reintroducing himself to Quimby. After leaving Fred, he stopped for a cold drink at the Burger Bucket drive-in and flirted very mildly with the waitress, who, despite several tattoos and piercings, looked no more than nineteen. She stood at the counter, smoking, trying to maintain her cool while whispering to the fry girl. Zack looked away, smiling at a squalling toddler in the next car until he recognized the child's mother, Liz Somebody from high school, who gaped at him with her mouth open. After the first moment of shock, she recovered enough to shoot him an impressively nasty evil eye.

He drove away, remembering that Liz had been one of Laurel's bridesmaids. And that there were six of them.

Enough for a posse.

Next he went to the lake. In another week the water would be warm enough for pleasant swimming, but even now there were several hardy bathers. Pale, fleshy bodies lined the sand like walruses basking in the sun. Little kids dashed in and out of the shallows, squealing and splashing, the lifeguard poised to take flight from his peeling white throne.

Zack parked and sat on the hood of his car. The water and sky were complementary shades of blue, drenched with so much sunlight his eyes began to water and he had to fish a pair of shades from his pocket. He smelled pine resin, warm tar. Hot sand. The medicinal odor of sunscreen and the indefinable dank, marshy tang of lake water.

Memories came in a flood. He'd been the lifeguard at Mirror Lake for four summers, from ages sixteen to twenty. An uncomplicated time. He remembered the slow roasting hours of midday, the usual teenage horseplay with his swim team buddies, the day Julia Knox had pranced across the sand in braids and a yellow bikini and he'd decided that she was the girl for him.

Zack grimaced. His life would have stayed uncomplicated if only they'd married. For a time, he'd thought that eventually they would...until Julia had come to him at the start of their junior year of college and confessed that she loved someone else. The worst part of it had been that he wasn't devastated by the news, not really. He and Julia...they'd never *truly* sparked. Not in the crackling, fiery way that burned hot enough to last a lifetime.

Zack stood up. Enough wallowing. Someone looked over and waved at him from a beach towel as he slammed the car door. He didn't stop. Gravel spit beneath the back wheels of the Jag as he peeled out of the parking lot like a hot-rodder.

He pulled together a bagful of groceries at the little mom-and-pop convenience store at the crossroads.

Mom was too myopic to see beyond her nose. Pop looked at Zack with a vague recognition; Zack was gone before it jelled.

The sun had dropped significantly lower in the sky by the time he returned home, its beams slanting through the green lacy screen of the willows. The grass looked like a velvet carpet. The buds on the rhododendron were on the verge of opening, but for now the pink petals were still tightly furled.

Turning into the drive, he almost clipped the mailbox. Several wan tulips lost their drooping heads beneath the left front wheel as he stepped hard on the brake and the car shuddered to an abrupt halt.

Cathy Timmerman was home.

He climbed from the Jag in a daze.

She was washing her car. In bare feet and denim cut-offs. With a sleeveless white T-shirt knotted below her breasts. Above a triangle of smooth abdomen, her pointed nipples pressed against the damp, clinging fabric. A thick, shiny ponytail bobbed at the back of her head when she stood abruptly with a sponge in one hand and a hose in the other, its spray wetting her cement driveway and the grass and then the tips of his athletic shoes as she slowly turned his way.

No Birkenstocks. No Mr. Magoo glasses. No baggy tent dress to disguise what he already knew to be a perfect figure.

Just a shy flicker of her lashes. A deep, deep breath.

And a welcoming, sweetly seductive smile.

4

"HI," SHE HEARD herself say almost normally, "I'm your neighbor, Cathy Timmerman." *Breathe.* "I've leased the Colton's house from Allie Spangler. And Kay Estress sold me her craft shop." *Keep talking. Be friendly.* "The place on Central Street? It's been renamed Scarborough Faire...."

"So I've been told," Zack said. His smile was kind, but there was something in his eyes, a mischievous glint perhaps, that made her remember every excruciating detail of the previous night's performance. "The grapevine, you know."

She blinked. "Oh. Right. The grapevine."

"You're wetting my shoes."

"I'm wetting your...?"

She looked down at herself, both hands clenching reflexively. Water spurted in a hard stream from the nozzle of the hose, blasting Zack's shoes and jeans. With a sharp exclamation, she threw away the hose and the sponge. The nozzle bounced on the pavement and landed trigger-down in the grass, its angle such that the spray fanned in a wide arc, dampening each of them with a fine mist.

"Yikes." Holding up her hands to block the spray, Cathy darted toward the hose.

"I'll get it," Zack said, reaching for it at the same instant. They grabbed it from opposite sides, making the cold water spurt through their fingers and onto their faces. Cathy let go. Zack redirected the spray, pressing the rusty trigger until finally it sprang back to the off position.

"Oh, gee, I'm sorry." She backed away a step, wiping at her chin. She'd soaked him. His face was streaming. His faded purple Kingpins T-shirt showed a darker splash pattern around the shoulders and his jeans—

Don't think about the jeans.

She already knew what he looked like in wet jeans.

"No problem," he said. "Just like old times. Allie's family left the garden hose snaked over the lawn all summer long." He grinned as he swiped the back of a wrist over his face. "I've been doused by this hose more times than I can remember."

The corners of his lips curled tightly when he grinned, carving dents in his cheeks. Not dimples. Just shallow dents. His eyes crinkled, too, and his warm brown irises were glinting at her again, sharing the joke, asking her to laugh. She was utterly charmed, but she couldn't quite manage a laugh. There was too much of him. Too much tall, handsome, strong, healthy male.

She had to say something. The group had coached her on how to engage him in conversation, but they hadn't foreseen a renegade water hose. It seemed prudent to jump straight to the invitation. "Umm, since you're so wet anyway, want to help me wash my car? You look like you'd be good at rubbing bumpers and..." *Heavens, this was embarrassing!* "...p-polishing headlights."

Surprise flashed across his face. His gaze dropped to her wet T-shirt, then quickly back up to her face. "Sure," he said, somewhat quizzically. "I'd be glad to rub your bumper."

Cathy's next line was supposed to be even more suggestive, but darned if she'd say it. There was no way on earth she'd seduce him sounding like a bad Mae West imitation. Instead she pointed at the front bumper. "Be my guest."

He kicked off his shoes and threw them into his own yard with a natural athletic grace, the muscles in his shoulders flexing beneath the clinging shirt. She blinked, realizing that wet T-shirts worked on both sexes.

"They were squidgy," he explained, intercepting her stare.

He's not squidgy.

"The shoes?" she blurted. "Sorry."

"They'll dry." He grinned again, making her brain swim, every rational thought slipping out of her grasp like an elusive goldfish. She was not worthy. Heck, she wasn't even capable.

He said, "So will the rest of me if I catch this last bit of sun."

She was still processing his meaning when he dragged his shirt off overhead, revealing a flat, hard abdomen and a muscular chest furred with hair a shade darker than that on his head. He wasn't deeply tanned, but his skin had a natural sun-kissed glow that told her he was accustomed to going shirtless. As he had last night.

Her fishbowl of a brain tipped sideways, emptying of all but the desire to feel his big hard muscular body pressed up against her own.

She backed up until she bumped into the sudsy car. Her eyes closed. Nothing Zack's old girlfriends had said could have prepared her for Heartbreak in the flesh!

Something soft and wet nudged her arm. Her eyes opened wide. Zack's face loomed before hers. "Your sponge," he said.

"Thank you." She took it, turning toward the car with a jerk. He knelt beside her with the hose and a rag and started working on the dingy bumper. *This is okay*, she thought, calming down as she methodically washed the hood, getting into the motion of it while she watched the top of Zack's head and his wide, muscled shoulders. *I'm doing fine.*

Then his elbow brushed against her bare leg. Her teeth clicked shut. Do not move, she told herself, battling her instinct to flee. *You are Woman, remember? Phenomenal, incomparable, confident Woman.*

She leaned forward, stretching across the hood, going for big, extravagant swipes that made her whole body sway. In her peripheral vision, she saw Zack setting back on his heels, his gaze glued to her behind. She became starkly aware of the brevity of her shorts and the wet patch that glued them to her buns. After four years in jumpers and pants, it was way too much exposure for her to handle on the first seduction attempt. Rome wasn't built in a day. Neither were femme fatales.

Zack put his hand on her calf.

She flinched. Badly. To him, the flinch might have seemed like a kick. "Oh, I'm sor—"

"You were about to put your foot in the bucket," he said, cutting off her apology.

"I'm such a klutz today."

"Hmm, I don't know about that. You were working up a good rhythm there, looking very..." His eyes burned a trail up her legs. "Graceful." The grin reappeared. "By the way—nice legs."

She gulped, her hands twisting nervously. Unfortunately, she was still holding the sponge. Dirty water rained down on Zack.

He popped up, shaking his head like a wet dog. "Got

me again," he said, forestalling another sputtered apology by ducking his head under the spray of the hose.

A curtain twitch drew her attention to the house. Allie and Julia were peering out at them, mouthing suggestions that Cathy had no hope of following. She waved them off as Zack straightened, wet to the roots, but clean. He raked both hands through his hair, leaving it standing on end. His brown eyes glowed with warmth. In contrast with a jaw shadowed by whiskers, his teeth were very white.

Lord, he was handsome.

Too handsome for her by far.

Burned by the Chad Timmerman experience, she didn't mix well with handsome men. They were accustomed to special treatment. She was a populist—every person had value, regardless of looks, wealth or social standing.

If this had been only a matter of Zack's looks, she could resist. She could adhere to the plan. But she knew Zack to be—or at least had *once* known him to be—kind and friendly and good-hearted as well, and that was complicating the deal. She'd been halfway in love with him for nearly twenty years. One little push—and the Heartbroken were after her, pushing hard—was all it would take. She'd be a goner.

"I can't get any wetter," he was saying. "So let's finish this car before the sun goes down."

I'm going down for the second time, she thought, hit with another wave of attraction as she watched him hose down the hood. *I am so going down....*

"Did I forgot to introduce myself?" he said above the sound of the pelting spray. "I'm Zack Brody." He offered his hand.

She took it. Her slippery palm slid against his. "I know."

His fingers closed over hers, holding on for a tantalizing few seconds before letting go. "The grapevine?"

"Yes." Of course he wouldn't recognize her. Most likely, he wouldn't remember her even if she gave him her maiden name. Cathy Bell had been only a tubby, awkward little girl he'd felt sorry for a very long time ago.

"Then you know I grew up here in Quimby. That's my family home next door."

Rays of sunlight streamed through the willow trees along the river, bouncing light off the gleaming chrome of her little two-door hatchback. Squinting, she ran the sponge along the door handles. "Uh-huh. Allie told me. You and she were neighbors all your lives."

Zack adjusted the nozzle, rinsing away the last of the suds. Sheets of clear water rippled and glistened, silky smooth. "Did she tell you what a funny little imp she was?"

"No." *I could have guessed that.* "But she told me what a royal pain *you* were."

He shrugged. "Probably."

"Where are your parents?" she asked, even though she knew. Like a squirrel, she'd gathered and stored away every little nugget of knowledge about Zack that had come her way in the past seven months. She knew that he'd earned a Good Conduct medal in the first grade. That he'd led the high school basketball team to a regional championship. That he'd moved to Chicago after college to take a prestigious job with an architectural firm, but had been granted an extended leave of absence after his brother's accident and the scandalous jilting.

"Couple of years ago, after their retirement, my parents and Allie's decided to buy a motor home together and take a tour of all fifty states. By the time they'd done twelve, the close quarters had become too close. They were fighting like cats and dogs."

Cathy chuckled. "Uh-oh."

"Finally they had a blowup—in an RV park in Independence, Missouri, smack-dab in the middle of the country. They'd been friends and neighbors for thirty years, but an argument over whose turn it was to empty the, uh, waste tank was the death of all that." Zack sprayed more water over the roof, shaking his head. "In order to save the last shreds of their friendship, they had to separate. So they sold the motor home right on the spot and split the money. The Coltons went to California. My parents went to Florida. And never the twain shall meet."

"That's a terrible story."

"Not so awful. My dad says they'll be friends again once waking up to the sight of Marlene Colton doing toe-touches in curlers and plaid pedal-pushers six inches from his nose fades from his memory."

Cathy cocked her head. "It's sort of sad. Two families, all those years, and now the houses are empty shells."

"No longer. We're here."

She went still under his direct gaze, and said, "That's so," with some caution.

He looked at the hose as if he'd forgotten it was still running, then shut it off. His smile was blinding. "The neighborhood's definitely looking up."

"You're planning to stay? Long-term?"

The smile faded. For the first time, his expression was less than forthright. "I thought I might."

"Oh."

She stepped aside as he walked around the car, his

bare feet slapping the wet pavement. Each tire got another blast from the hose. By his face she knew he was absorbed in a private struggle. "You must know about the wed—" He stopped, frowning. "My broken engagement to Laurel Barnard?"

"I heard things."

"Not pleasant things, I assume."

"Well, no. Laurel owns the dress shop next door to me. She's..." Cathy plucked at the front of her damp shirt, forgetting all about her mission of seduction. Zack sounded wary, not brash. Not glib. "She's talked."

He wiped his feet on the grass. "Then my reputation's mud with you."

Her eyes widened. He cared what she thought of him? "Not with me," she said. "The townspeople may be another matter. But as for me, I—uh—I—" Zack's gaze had swung up to her face, snagging her voice. She squared her shoulders, trying to get ahold of herself. To be honest and fair. The Zack she'd known deserved at least that much. "I don't like to judge a person. Any person. Certainly not unless I've heard both sides."

"That's good to hear." He dropped the coiled hose in the grass and came toward her, arms akimbo, chest... immense. Layered with hairy muscle. She could smell his warm skin. The scent was muskily tantalizing. "I'm glad we're neighbors, Cathy Timmerman."

She smiled a fluttery smile, hoping to pass off her solemn vow as no more than a friendly gesture. "Well, I don't own any plaid pedal-pushers. But I'll try to warn you before I do my morning exercises."

"Just close the curtains and we'll be fine."

"Close the—" Her throat seized up.

"What's the saying?" Zack started to touch her arm,

then stopped himself. Her skin prickled. "Something about closed curtains making good neighbors?"

He knew. And he knew *she* knew. Cathy gritted her teeth against the excruciating humiliation. Her nude doppelganger might as well be bellydancing between them.

"That would be 'good fences,'" she said, straining for normalcy, "but I get your meaning. I'll be sure to keep my curtains closed from now on." She couldn't stand it. Couldn't hold still for his provocative perusal. Certainly couldn't volley with the sexy *bon mots* the Heartbroken had suggested.

She mumbled something about lemonade and ran for the house.

"It's not necessary on my account," Zack called after her.

Cathy seriously doubted he meant her offer of a beverage.

"WHAT WERE YOU DOING?" Allie screeched as soon as Cathy slammed the door behind herself.

"Hush. Zack will hear you." Julia peeked out the window. "Uh-oh. He's coming toward the house."

Cathy bolted for the kitchen, leaving damp footprints on the living room carpet. "I offered him a cold drink."

"It's okay, it's okay," Julia said, following her. "He's only putting away the hose." She shut the window over the sink.

"Was that supposed to be playful?" Allie stood in the center of the cheerful but rundown kitchen, sounding belligerent. "Because it looked like a drowning attempt."

Cathy closed her ears and opened the ancient, round-shouldered fridge. "Where's that pitcher of lemonade?"

"Maybe you forgot," Allie said. "You're supposed to *entice* him."

"She's doing fine." Julia took two tall glasses from a knotty-pine cupboard. "Very natural."

"If at least you'd giggled when you squirted him—" Allie cracked the ice trays "—you could have gotten a water fight going. Which would have ended with wet T-shirts and slick skin and...hoo-ha, daddy!" Her eyebrows waggled suggestively as she dropped three cubes in each glass.

Julia scoffed. "They're not teenagers."

Cathy let out a sigh. "Standing out there for twenty minutes in teensy cutoffs and bare feet was bad enough," she said, untying her T-shirt and fanning it out so it would dry a little faster. "But then when Allie came out and sprayed down my shirt..." She winced. "I felt like a reject from a Playboy video."

"Zack noticed, didn't he?"

"How could he not?" Cathy concentrated on pouring lemonade over the crackling ice. "The setup wasn't subtle."

"You should have worked it more," Allie said.

"I tried the bumpers-and-headlights line." Cathy pushed away the memory of her awkward delivery. "It was awful."

"Told you," said Julia to Allie.

"Hey. It always works on Fred. I haven't washed a car on my own since we met."

The glasses were wet with condensation. Carefully Cathy wiped up a drop of spilled lemonade; ants were a problem. "You're the type who can say things like that and come off looking cute and saucy. I sounded as wooden as a porn actress."

Allie giggled. "Does that mean he didn't offer to lube the pistons and shafts?"

"Heavens, no."

"But you two were talking," Julia said. "That's good."

"He told me about his and Allie's parents and the motor home."

"Oh, yeah. The honey tank controversy," Allie said with a roll of her eyes. "Doesn't sound too romantic."

"What else?" asked Julia.

"Ohhh..." Cathy didn't care to go into their discussion of the broken engagement. The moment felt too personal to her, especially when she remembered Zack's guarded expression. "Nothing important. We chatted."

Julia nodded. "He's already interested."

Cathy's stomach dropped. "How can you tell?"

"Female intuition." Julia smiled. "Plus, I know him well enough to see the signs. You must have picked up on them yourself, Cath."

Allie's eyes narrowed and her features compressed, nearly making her long nose meet her upper lip. "What signs?"

Cathy shook her head. "I didn't notice any signs. Except the one that said he thinks I'm a total dweeb."

"Doesn't matter." Allie suddenly turned and slapped the counter. "You look good in shorts. That's enough." She flicked a dead ant onto the linoleum.

"Not for Zack," Julia said quietly.

"Still riding the Heartbreak bandwagon?" Allie flung back her head, her eyes shooting emerald sparks. "He was going to marry Laurel, for pity's sake. *Laurel.*"

Julia shifted uncomfortably. "Laurel's a friend."

"Laurel would have stabbed you in the back without a regret when it came to Zack Brody," Allie charged.

"You know she was trying for him even when you two were together."

"Of course I knew," Julia murmured.

"How that man could propose marriage to such a land shark in the first place I'll never under—"

The front door opened. "Cathy?" Zack called. "Need any help in there?"

"No-o-o," she warbled, her voice too shrill and panicky. "Stay where you are. I'm coming!"

The front door closed; the back door opened. Gwendolyn Case poked her head inside. "How's it going?" she said in the husky voice that was her version of a whisper. "I saw Zack sitting out front, so I snuck around the back. Is he showing any signs of crumbling at Cathy's feet?"

The other women hushed her while Cathy grabbed up the glasses. This was a farce. The only hope she had of attracting Zack was to relax and be herself, albeit with a prettied-up appearance, and she couldn't do that with the Wednesday nighters hanging on her every word. "Listen, guys," she pleaded, "can you all just leave? This is weird enough for me as it is. I don't need the audience."

"Of course." Julia's expression was sympathetic. "We'll tiptoe out the back as soon as you and Zack are occupied."

Allie took Cathy by the shoulders and shoved her toward the living room. "Just remember to play with the ice cubes. Rub one of them on your lips. Along your throat. You'll have Zack panting like the dog that he is."

I'd sooner leap off an iceberg, Cathy thought, but she headed for the door with the lemonade, leaving the women alternately hissing, squabbling and shushing themselves in the kitchen.

"Got company?" Zack said when she stepped outside. He'd been sitting on the front steps, but he rose to hold the screen door for her.

"Um, not exactly. A neighbor dropped by to borrow sugar." Not bad. Sounded like the ideal small-town excuse.

"Mrs. Beringer, I suppose."

"How'd you guess?"

"Then she must have cured her diabetes," Zack said mildly.

Trap! "Umm. I wouldn't know. She's making cupcakes for the bake sale." In Quimby, there was always a bake sale on the horizon.

Luckily Zack didn't pursue the subject. He took a lemonade and waited for her to sit. The guy had manners. He would have even pulled out her chair, but the concrete steps weren't budging. "You finished the car," she said brightly, covering her disappointment that he'd also put his shirt back on.

He drank like a man, with gusto and a satisfied *ahhh*. He wiped his chin with the neck of his shirt. "There are still the windows to do."

Her glance was shy. "Thanks for helping."

"I didn't do such a good job..." he said sadly.

"Oh, no, really—"

"Didn't even start a water fight," he finished, looking at her with raised brows. He licked a bead of liquid from the corner of his mouth.

Her face warmed. She thrust her nose into the lemonade and slurped noisily. Had Zack heard them talking in the kitchen? Possibly. But not likely. He didn't strike her as the devious type. If he'd heard, he'd ask outright what was going on.

'Course, he *had* tried to trap her on the Mrs. Beringer excuse.

And she'd read Chad Timmerman all wrong.

History could repeat itself with Zack. He was, after all, an infamous jilter of brides.

A smooth operator.

A legendary heartbreaker.

Tread cautiously, Cathy advised herself. To Zack, she smiled and said, "Well, we're not teenagers. I doubt a water fight was necessary."

"I disagree. Play is as much a necessity as work."

"Humph. It doesn't pay the rent."

He smiled gently and shook his head, then turned his face away from hers to gaze across the yards. Water droplets glistened in the lush June grass. Squirrels scurried from branch to branch in the white oaks that overhung the street; their leafy shadows dappled the pavement in constantly shifting patterns. Big white clouds with purple edges raced each other across the deepening sky.

Cathy was on tenterhooks, waiting for Zack to say something significant. She felt as if she might burst out of her skin. As though she could shed all her inhibitions and dance barefoot in the wet grass, singing at the top of her voice.

"It fills the heart," he said at last. "It feeds the soul."

"Fun?"

"In a manner of speaking. 'Enjoyment' sounds better. Living life to its fullest."

The cubes in Cathy's glass knocked together; her

hands were shaking. "Isn't that the definition of hedonism?"

A smile slanted across Zack's lips. "You have a problem with hedonism?"

The surprising answer popped into her head: *Not lately.*

But it would be safer to spout one of her father's work-ethic credos.

Cathy didn't let herself answer either way, literally holding her tongue between her teeth as she reminded herself that she was supposed to be seducing Zack, not engaging him in a philosophical discussion. Her one extended experience with living *la vida loca* had ended badly. She'd used that as an excuse to retreat back into her shell. The notion that she'd gone about it in the wrong way had occurred since then. Truth was, Zack had arrived at the optimal moment, when she was ready to try again. Older and wiser.

Let's hope so, because here goes nothing.

"Hedonism has its place." She fixed a Mona Lisa smile upon her lips and looked at him from the corner of her eyes, lashes lowered. "I've been known to thrive on pleasure...."

Zack set aside their lemonade glasses. He brushed his fingertips over her arm, inciting a delicious tingling sensation. "Would that be pleasures of the flesh?"

"Among others."

"A woman after my own heart."

She forgot the agenda. Her chin tilted up instead of down. Her lips thinned instead of pouting. "From what I hear, it's my heart that's in danger. You don't offer your own that easily...*Heartbreak.*"

Grinning sheepishly, he squeezed the tip of his nose

between thumb and forefinger several times. An unthinking, fidgety gesture that surprised her, coming from the man whose moves were supposed to be as smooth as glass. She felt herself softening. Another unplanned reaction.

"My reputation has been greatly exaggerated," he said. The end of his nose was pink.

"Really. I am devastated."

His brows went up. The grin morphed back into confidence. "Hmm. We can't have that."

She swayed closer, brushing against him. "There are certain expectations that must be met."

"Or else?"

Her gaze lifted. "I will feel terribly left out."

He studied her face. For a moment, she thought he might recognize something—some long-forgotten remnant of the pudgy, forsaken schoolgirl she'd been, but then his expression smoothed out and they were back into familiar territory. He clasped her hand. She resisted the swoon and shudder of her reaction, determined to stay in charge.

"I'd rather keep you apart, Cathy. Unique and separate. A singular woman."

Her lids lowered. *He probably says that to all the girls,* she cautioned herself, when what she wanted was to believe him with all her heart.

My, how skilled he was!

What, other than his too-glib words, made her think she could ever be the *one*?

"How special," she purred into the warmth building between them.

Zack's eyes darkened. "You don't believe me."

"Oh, but I do. For the moment."

He propped her chin on the tips of his fingers, tilting her face toward his. "Then let this be a moment that lasts forever," he said with all the polish she'd been told to expect, his touch sending shivers through her with an ease she recognized, but was nonetheless entirely unprepared for.

She made a small unintelligible sound in her throat when he leaned even closer. Their breath intermingled. Her lips parted.

He did not kiss them.

He licked them...tracing the shape of her mouth with the wet velvet tip of his tongue, as if tasting a rare treat that must be savored as slowly and as sensuously as possible. A desperate desire swelled within her.

He lapped her bottom lip, making it bobble. He touched the dent above her upper lip, then licked horizontally along the underside of it until he reached the corner, where his tongue lingered deliciously until she had to open her mouth to catch at her breath and then...! Oh, heaven, then he was *inside* her mouth, his tongue hot and firm and urgent—a probing blade that sucked the hesitation right out of her. Her heart pounded wildly. She pressed her mouth to his, her arms wrapping around his shoulders. In the deepening passion of their kiss, all calculation and constraint was lost, like the sign at the entrance of an unearthly portal: Abandon Control All Ye Who Enter Here.

It was the best kiss of her life.

While she clutched at handfuls of his shirt, his hungry mouth found her jaw, her throat, the curve where her neck met her shoulder. He sniffed deeply as his lips sought her ear, peppering tiny kisses into its swirls, nuzzling behind it, rooting for every shred of pleasure they might share. He wound her ponytail around his hand and used it to angle her head at the perfect slant as his mouth descended onto hers, his face so filled with desire, her eyes grew round.

"Unh," she blurted. "Stop." Over Zack's shoulder, she saw Allie, Julia and Gwen scurry through a neighbor's yard. Allie, turning back to look, stopped short at the sight of the clinch. A faint "Hot damn!" floated across the yards.

Cathy pressed her palms flat over Zack's ears as if she needed to hold his head in place. And she kissed him—a loud smack of a kiss that was not in the least romantic or seductive.

"I have to go," she said, unmoving. Julia had grabbed onto Allie's arm and was towing her away.

Zack pried her hands off the sides of his head. He pressed a warm kiss onto each palm.

Her fingers curled around the lingering sensation like a child who'd snatched blown kisses from the air. "I really do—I really must—"

"Have dinner with me."

She gulped. "Tonight?"

"Yes." His eyes were bright, fixed on hers with an interest that seemed genuine. And intense.

"No," she said, panicking at the thought of being unprepared. Besides, the women had told her to play it cagey—not to be too readily available.

"Tomorrow?" he suggested.

"Yes, tomorrow."

He touched her cheek, said "Yes, tomorrow," as if she'd granted him his greatest wish.

She was discombobulated, but very pleased.

Zack stood, bent to kiss the top of her head, then

turned and sped with a bounding, joyous grace through their twin driveways and up the steps of the Brody house. At the door he stopped to throw a wave at Cathy, his smile bright as the sun, and then he was gone and she was left to blink at the space he'd filled with an overwhelming quantity of warmth and charm and pure male sex appeal.

She was blinded.

Stunned.

Thoroughly smitten.

5

AT TEN MINUTES to eight o'clock the next evening, Zack was shaving in the steamy, blue-tiled bathroom he'd shared for many years with his brother, never mind the lack of elbow room. It was a narrow space, built into a closet during a renovation of the 1940s-era house, with stainless steel fixtures and a shower tucked beneath the slanted ceiling.

Fortunately, he and Adam had always been close, despite their constant tussling and teasing. From the time they were little tykes, their father had made it clear that it was Zack's job to watch out for his fearless younger brother. Though Zack couldn't have done less, he'd come to wonder if his steady accountability had given Adam too much freedom.

Sure, Adam was a risk taker. He had the benefit of a built-in safety net.

Tonight, however, brotherly concern was not foremost in Zack's mind, especially since they'd talked on the phone earlier in the day. Adam had reported on his progress with the physiologist; Zack had tread lightly around the subject of his cautious return to Quimby. Laurel Barnard, no longer an issue, but still a sore subject, had not been mentioned.

"Damn." Zack lowered the razor and cocked his head at the mirror. A bright red bead had appeared on the underside of his jaw.

Not a *sore* subject. But an annoying one.

He dabbed the blood with a tissue, then dug through the medicine cabinet, looking for a styptic pencil. An open box of condoms fell into the sink. Adam's, surely. Too bad he hadn't used them with Laurel.

Double damn. Zack shook his head. "Not tonight," he said to his reflection. Nicer to think of Cathy Timmerman.

His mouth turned up. Cathy was a strange mix of womanly wiles and awkward bashfulness. He sensed a story there. The thought of slowly plucking her petals to get to the sweet secret nectar at the heart of her piqued his interest to a surprising degree. Though he'd more than had his fill of manipulative women, Cathy didn't strike him as devious. Just complicated.

Zack took the box out of the sink, hesitated, then tore one of the packets off the strip and pocketed it. Grinned at himself in the mirror. Pocketed two more.

He'd always been an optimist.

He finished shaving, toweled off, and patted a slight hint of aftershave onto his smoothed skin. Whistling, he went to the bedroom to put on his shirt, fresh from the dry cleaner's.

Fred Spangler sat on the edge of the bed, watching a baseball game on TV, his legs spread wide, his gut hanging over his unsnapped jeans. "Pretty boy," he said sarcastically, without removing his gaze from the screen, where the Cubs' starting pitcher was being drilled in only the third inning. Without benefit of Novocaine.

"Pretty girl," Zack countered, thinking of the curve of Cathy's behind as she leaned over the car hood. The solid promise in her voice when she said she hadn't judged him.

"Maybe if you peel the tent off her." Fred glanced at

his wristwatch and chuckled. "And I'm figuring you'll be doing 'zackly that 'round about three hours from now."

Feeling like it was his first date all over again, Zack removed his button-down shirt and put on a plain black crewneck instead. It was stretchy and lightweight—nonbinding; he could breathe. "Cathy might have something to say about that."

"She's a rookie. Had to call in Allie and Julia for reinforcements." Fred shook his head. "Naw. Cathy might be a Goody Two-shoes, but she hasn't got a chance against the patented Heartbreak charm."

Take me, her mouth had said. But her eyes had been wary.

"We're going out to dinner," Zack said. "That's all."

"Jerome's." Fred was distracted, absorbed again in the game.

"Pardon?"

"Allie told me to tell you to take Cathy to Jerome's."

"What's wrong with The Potting Shed?" Zack asked, though he'd planned on Jerome's all along.

Fred waved a pinky. "More romanick. Tra-la-la."

"Romantic," Zack ruminated, rehanging his ties. He pulled a tan suede sports coat off a hanger in the color-coded closet. "Why's Allie pulling strings?"

She'd dropped by that morning, first to hug him, then to slug him. A half-hearted reading of the riot act had followed, but their time apart—and her patented disapproval of Laurel—had blunted much of the scolding. After they'd caught up, Allie had been highly interested in hearing about his dinner date. He'd taken that for her normal nosiness.

So Allie and Julia were next door, offering dating tips,

filling Cathy in on all his misdeeds? He wasn't sure he cared for the sound of that.

"...THEN WHEN HE TRIES to kiss you—"

"Stop!" Cathy laid aside the book—*Architecture of the New Millennium*—that Faith had checked out of the library. Her mind was already awhirl with the advice and instructions they'd been pelting at her. It refused to hold even one more helpful hint.

"Don't be so darned eager next time," Allie said, picking up where Laurel had been interrupted. She was carefully arranging Cathy's hair in a chignon at the back of her head. "I thought you were going to crawl into his lap. Get some self-control, girlfriend."

"Says you, Allie." Julia reclined on the bed heaped with rejected outfits, watching the proceedings with a caustic eye. "You haven't been submitted to the powerful allure of Zack's kiss."

Faith, sitting beside the cluttered dressing table with stars in her eyes, sighed with longing. She'd studied every step of Cathy's transformation.

"Says *you.* I was the first girl he ever kissed," Allie insisted hotly, tugging Cathy's hair with enough vigor to make her wince. "That counts."

"Childish pecks?" Laurel's laugh dismissed Allie's experience as insignificant. She folded a rejected outfit into a silver-gray Couturier box, looking smug.

"We played Spin The Bottle," Gwen chimed in from her post at the window, most heartily. "And lemme tell ya, Zack already knew exactly what he was doing."

Laurel's lashes flicked. "But you've *only* had his adolescent kisses." Gwen flushed, but couldn't argue. "Julia and I have applicable knowledge of the depth of his many *manly* charms."

Laurel's smooth superiority was palling. Gwen and Allie stared daggers at her. Faith's eyes were like marbles.

"What is this, a competition?" Julia asked, which was what Cathy had been thinking. "I'm sure we can all agree that Zack's kisses are hard to resist."

"But resist them Cathy must," Laurel said.

"For sure." Allie's face was grim as she uncapped a bottle of hair spray.

Julia sat up. "Not initially."

"Zack must first be drawn into the web," Laurel instructed as she scoured the pupil from head to toe. Instead of an incipient Spiderwoman, Cathy felt like a frog undergoing dissection. "We want him well and truly besotted."

"*Then* she says no." Allie sprayed without warning. Cathy winced and slammed shut her eyes.

Gwen huffed. "Isn't it kind of impossible to play hard to get when she's already sucked the guy's tonsils?"

Cathy's eyes shot open. *Thanks a lot, Gwen.* She dropped her chin in abject embarrassment, but Allie gave the chignon a tug, forcing her gaze up from the new cosmetics littered across the surface of the dressing table. Cathy confronted herself in the mirror, awed by the subtle, sophisticated effect of Laurel's skillfully applied makeup. *That's not me. Not plain, sensible Cathy Bell Timmerman.*

Suddenly she was thrust back into her college years, when she'd taken advantage of the school gym and dietician and finally dropped the extra pounds that were the result of a lifetime of comfort food. Newly svelte and experiencing positive male attention for the first time, she'd been persuaded to join her roommates on their man-trolling expeditions at local clubs. Though she'd been terribly awkward at first, she'd soon learned to ape her friends' hoochie-coochie style of dress and sassy attitude. Like them, she'd taken to calling her makeup "war paint" and her stream of admirers "conquests." She'd been profligate with the currency of finally being a desirable female in a world that placed its highest value on appearance.

Only after her and Chad's elopement and downward slide into marital discord did she realize just how shallow her life had become, and how much she missed the old Cathy. Eventually she'd managed to correct her mistakes and return to her true self. That short-lived glittering butterfly of a woman was not someone she'd ever expected to revisit.

Yet here came the Heartbroken, trying to send her back there, in a sense. They could call it striking a blow for womankind, but it was still revenge and it was... wrong.

Even though her personal motive was pure? she wondered, reprimanding herself for being wishy-washy. She needed to pick a position and stick with it.

"This isn't right," she said, freshly appalled by how easily she'd gone along with the scheme. All because she wanted Zack.

"Hoo, boy, here comes Heartbreak," Gwen said from the window, overriding Cathy's soft-spoken protest. "My Lord, that man has zippety-doo-dah to spare!"

The next few minutes passed in a blur. The women all ran to the window to gape at Zack. Next they descended on Cathy, giving her no opening to back out. She was primped and fluffed, then hustled downstairs, dozens of last-minute suggestions flying in one ear and out the other. The doorbell had rung twice. When Zack knocked, Gwen forced Cathy's frozen hand onto the doorknob. The women retired to a vantage point behind the swinging kitchen door. They were staying; they still had a romantic seduction scene to set.

Cathy opened the door.

"Let's go," she said, barely registering Zack's greeting.

"Don't you want to put the flowers in a vase?" he said. Despite the treacherous high-heeled sandals Laurel had insisted upon, Cathy was down the steps and half-way to his car.

"Flowers?" She stopped and turned, thinking, *Don't let it be roses.* Laurel had once gone on and on about how Zack had brought her roses when he proposed and how the wedding was rife with them, including a carpet of rose petals all the way up the aisle. It was something Laurel couldn't forgive—the waste of all those expensive roses.

Zack walked toward Cathy, holding a small but thick bundle of green leaves wrapped in lavender tissue. Cathy peered closer. "Oh, Zack. Lily of the Valley. I love them. How did you guess?"

"No guessing involved," he said. "I've yet to meet a woman who didn't love flowers of any sort."

"Of course." She buried her scowl in the cluster of delicate white flowers, inhaling their lovely fragrance. According to the Heartbroken, Zack brought flowers to all his women. It had been another area of contention and one-upsmanship between them.

"Thanks," she said. "Let's go." Perhaps he did deserve to know what it felt like to be the cheese who stood alone.

He blinked. "All right. Let's go."

Quimby was a small town, both in population and in area. A person, even one without the benefit of a fancy

Jaguar sports car, could drive from one end of town to the other in a matter of minutes. Cathy was still adjusting to the rare experience of being out with a stunning man in an equally stunning vehicle with sumptuous classical music pouring from the speakers when they pulled up outside of Jerome's, Quimby's finest restaurant. The engine cut off; the lush music stopped abruptly.

Cathy's heart sank. Allie had warned her. This was where Zack took all his women for their "big" date. Jerome's was an impressive sight, a restaurant converted from a solidly built bank. The windows were tall and arched, the facade graced with the kind of carved details modern buildings lacked.

Silence.

Zack was staring at the large cream brick building with a peculiar expression, his hand on the knob of the gear shift. Cathy cleared her throat. "Are we going in?"

His fingers flexed. "I have a better idea."

Pizza, Chianti and an offbeat movie. According to Julia, it was his favorite "spur of the moment" date.

"Let's go in for a drink," he said, leaving the car and coming around to open her door before continuing, "because this may take a while."

She swung her legs out, knees together. One of her high heels skidded on the pavement. He offered his hand, saving her from a graceless exit. Standing, she found her eyes on a level with his mouth, one advantage of three-inch heels. He had a very nice mouth—perfectly drawn. She could copy its curved lines for a calligraphy lesson.

His fingers linked with hers as they followed another couple into the restaurant through a massive arched Gothic entrance. She caught herself wishing that she'd never met the Wednesday nighters, that she and Zack were on a regular date—no baggage, no subtext, no angst.

Get real, she told herself. *There's always baggage. Sometimes it's Samsonite and sometimes it's Louis Vuitton, but it's always heavy.*

And sooner or later, it had to be opened.

Not tonight, she decided, accepting a stool at the bar and a glass of red wine while Zack held a murmured conversation with the maître d'. A folded bill exchanged hands, so neatly done she almost missed it. A smooth operator, for certain. She sipped, wondering what he was up to.

He joined her at the bar, lady-killer suave in black linen and tan suede. He was alarmingly attractive, as well groomed and highly polished as a show horse, exuding good breeding and powerful vitality with every gesture, every breath.

"Are you going to keep me in the dark?" she asked.

He laid his hand over hers atop the bar. "I'd like to."

She flushed. "You know what I meant."

"Hmm. Don't you like surprises?"

"Not very. I might be the creative type, but I'm also a planner." Her father's influence cast a wide net.

"Not tonight." He rubbed his fingertips over her knuckles. She tensed, certain he'd comment. Lotion and a manicure were not enough to gild the lily of her working hands.

He lifted her hand to his mouth and kissed the roughened knuckles.

The warmth in her face slid like a blob of butter into the pit of her stomach. *Down for the third time*, she thought. *Without so much as a struggle.*

"Tell me about your plans," he said in a smoke-and-honey baritone that might have soothed her nervousness if she hadn't been listening to his words.

Suddenly vehement, she shook her head, insisting at a high pitch, "I don't have a plan."

"No?"

She nodded agreement. *Not tonight* was getting to be the theme of the evening. Here's hoping she had strength to follow through with it when Zack began applying goodnight kisses.

No, no, it was *she* who'd be directing the action. *She* was the seductress.

Not easy to remember when every time he looked at her with his warm chocolate-brown eyes all she wanted was to melt into his arms and stay there for the rest of her life.

"I'm enjoying myself too much to settle down yet," she said, determinedly shutting the lid on the private dreams tucked away inside her heart. Though she hoped for a husband and kids, she'd already decided that if it didn't happen, she could lead a happy and contented life anyway. She wasn't husband-hungry...at least not at thirty.

"Oh, really," Zack said.

Watching him from beneath her lashes, she drew the wrap up along her bare arm. Slowly. "So many men, so little time."

He seemed puzzled, but intrigued. He put his arm around her shoulders and leaned closer. "Never mind those other men. Concentrate on me."

She blinked several times. "You forget I'm a craftsperson. My powers of concentration are...highly developed. And I linger over details with utmost care."

"I like the sound of—" His voice broke off. "Do you need a tissue?"

"No, thank you." She touched a pinkie to the corner of one eye, pulling the skin taut to wipe away a tear. "You were saying?"

His hand slid along her back. "I was saying that—" He stopped again. "Your eyes are watering. Does the smoke bother you?" They were seated at the end of the bar closest to the smoking section, separated only by a phalanx of potted palms and ferns. A faint odor of cigarette smoke permeated the air. "I'll ask for a table."

Some seductress. She stood and took her tiny pouch purse off the bar. "That won't be necessary. Excuse me, please. I'll be right back."

She found the bathroom, winced at her red, watery eyes, and removed the contact lenses. Dabbing with a tissue took care of the residue of tears, but removed most of her eyeliner as well. Laurel would call her a hopeless case. "Be that as it may," Cathy murmured to her out-of-focus reflection, "Zack seems to approve." She wrapped herself in cashmere and felt along the solid marble wall until she found the doorknob.

Zack was waiting with a filled wicker hamper when she returned, having negotiated her way through the airy, high-ceilinged restaurant with only a minor amount of squinting. They returned to the car and were soon out of Quimby proper, heading southeast on a bumpy two-lane road that led into farmland and forest preserves if one kept going.

Zack didn't get that far. He turned the car toward the empty beach parking lot.

"Ah, the lake," Cathy said, clued in at last. Having missed out on the summer season, she was not as familiar with Mirror Lake as she was with other Quimby hot spots. But she'd been out here a few times to enjoy the scenery, often enough to be familiar with the layout that consisted of a peeling white gazebo, a small children's playground and a wooden shack with red-and-white striped awnings that housed changing rooms and a snack bar.

The pale sand beach curved in an arc, lapped by a large lake shaped like a flattened egg. Though a light breeze sighed through the trees, the rustling leaves and creaking branches only served to emphasize the silence and isolation of the place. The air was balmy. Moonlight glistened on the dark surface of the water. Cathy's antennae quivered. Zack sure knew how to pick his romantic nightspots.

"You might want to take off your shoes," he said.

She'd expected the gazebo, but he was tromping off through the sand with the hamper from Jerome's. He put it down near the edge of the lake and turned back to see if she'd followed, watching her as he slipped out of his shoes and socks.

Cathy hesitated. A picnic in the sand? Okay, she could do that.

Zack came back for her. "I can carry you." His eyes twinkled when he said it, but she knew he'd follow through willingly enough.

"I'll walk, thanks," she said, stooping to unbuckle her sandals. Being lifted in Zack's arms was more than she could handle. Even the mere mention had made her stomach stir with nervous excitement.

When she stepped into the soft, dimpled sand, he was there to steady her with a hand on her elbow. "It's cold," she said, her toes curling.

He swooped her up. "I wouldn't want you to catch a chill," he said, looking down into her face and chuckling. "Close your mouth. You'll catch flies instead of cold."

She clamped her lips together. Never in her life had she been carried by a man—not as a child by her stern father, and not even over the threshold, because Chad had been too tipsy on their wedding night in Vegas. She had half a mind to wriggle away, but Zack's arms felt strong around her and his chest was solid and so very warm that the episode was over before she could summon so much as a token protest.

He deposited her in a row boat that sat marooned on the wet sand, added the hamper, then gave the awkward craft a tremendous push so they were launched into the water before he clambered aboard.

Cathy hugged her legs. Zack's unquestioning confidence and manly proficiency were attractive qualities, she must admit. He wasn't authoritative in a way that made her bristle, like her father. He simply...took charge.

It was pleasant, watching him row, being lulled by the gentle splash of water against wood and the lovely, starry night, but finally she had to ask, "Where *are* we going?"

"The best dining spot in Quimby."

She looked around. A raft loomed over her left shoulder. This is a new one, she thought. Wait till the women hear about Heartbreak's current method.

But I don't want to tell them. Zack grabbed hold of the raft to steady the boat while Cathy secured the painter to a rusty hasp, mooring them in place. They shared a "good teamwork" smile. *I won't tell them,* she decided. *This is just for me.*

And Zack.

He reached for her hand.

She gave it.

Knowing she was sunk.

ZACK LAY on his back, staring up at the night sky because staring for too long and too closely at Cathy might give her reservations about his purpose when, really, he'd be happy just to look at her for hours on end. At present, however, she didn't appear to be uneasy. She was prone on her stomach beside him, atop the white linen tablecloth the restaurant had provided, plucking at the chocolate-dipped fruit that was their dessert. Her knees were bent; both feet waved in the air, crossing and uncrossing. Her soles flashed white in the moonlight, and her toes were small and pink like tiny curled shrimp.

Odd. It was possible to be both incredibly aroused and totally relaxed at the same time. He wondered how she'd react if he kissed her instep, but was far too lazy to make the move.

They'd had a good conversation over dinner. She'd teased him about his lifeguard summers, making bad *Baywatch* jokes and praising his famous rescue of Faith Fagan, before segueing into her years as a Navy brat moving from port to port. Some reacted to the lifestyle by developing an outgoing and independent personality, but she confessed to turning inward, becoming a loner, developing the creative skills that were now her métier.

She seemed to know all about his childhood. The grapevine, he supposed. Allie and Gwen and Laurel. It wasn't that interesting, anyway. His upbringing was so normal and healthy, a 1950s television series could have been filmed in the Brody household.

The dramatic turns had come recently. *Runaway Groom*, starring Heartbreak Brody.

Cathy selected a chocolate-covered strawberry. "You

must really rate with the people at Jerome's to have coaxed this spread out of them on a whim."

"I'm a charming guy." He crossed his arms behind his head.

Her brows went up. "Ha! I saw, you know. It was bribery."

He smiled. "The money may have helped." She nibbled at the plump berry and nibbled, nibbled at his restraint.

"I hear you're a very good customer."

"True. I have an in with the owner."

Her tongue flicked out to catch a droplet of juice. "Oh?"

"Jerry Crockett's a friend. When he wanted to turn the old bank building into a restaurant, but was on a tight budget, I designed the renovations as a college project."

"That's incredible. It's a fantastic interior. All that marble and gilt. Turning the vault into a private dining room and wine cellar was so clever."

"So you've already been there."

"Of course." She looked across the water for a moment, then solemnly met his eyes. "You're not the only guy who knows a romantic possibility when he sees one."

He was bereft at the idea of her out with another man, and his dismay came out as a blunt question. "Who?"

"I shouldn't kiss and tell."

"In Quimby, everyone kisses and tells. There's no other recourse."

She tossed her hair. "Then it should be simple enough to find out if you really must know."

"You're a sassy wench."

Her mouth made an *O*.

He went up on his elbow, reached into the dish and

popped one of the rich, chocolate-covered cherries into
the provocative *O*. "Told you," he said. "Keep your
lovely mouth closed or else..."

Her teeth came together, snapping the fruit off at the
stem.

"Or elth...?" she repeated through the decadent
mouthful of chocolate and cherry.

"I'll be forced to kiss it shut." Lord have mercy. Her
lips were stained red. They pouted as she chewed, so full
and ripe the desire to kiss her rushed through him like a
white-water river. He hadn't felt so strongly about a
woman in a long time. Maybe forever. And still he held
back, uncertain why, his heart thudding in his chest.

She swallowed. "Wrong-o, Heartbreak."

He touched the stem to her chin, slowly drawing it
back and forth. An excruciating anticipation filled the
space between them, swelling like a balloon on the point
of bursting.

Cathy inhaled through her nose. Her lids lowered, the
long black lashes brushing her cheeks. "Well, Zack...in
my experience—" her voice cracked "—it's far better to
kiss a mouth *open*."

Before he could answer she snapped at the stem, drag-
ging it out of his fingers. It disappeared between her
lips, the suction of the action putting hollows into her
cheeks. Her jaw worked back and forth. He started to
say something, something inane, surely, but she stopped
him with a raised finger.

He waited.

Her eyes narrowed in concentration. Her lips pursed,
utterly kissable.

The tip of her tongue appeared for an instant, then
vanished. Finally, with a small wet sound, she inserted a

forefinger between her puckered lips and withdrew the cherry stem.

It had been knotted.

Knotted.

He covered his astonishment with a bark of laughter that echoed across the vast lake. "What an exceptional woman," he said, grabbing her face in his hands and kissing her soundly—jokingly. "But dare I ask?"

She broke into giggles even before he'd stopped kissing her. "Do you remember a show called *Twin Peaks*?" He shook his head. "Well, my best friend and I saw it when we were teens. There was an actress who did that thing with a stem, and we thought it was so neat! We practiced—and practiced—" Smothered laughter against the back of her hand. "Ohh," she said, gasping. She wiped her eyes. "Of course we had no real idea of the implications!"

"You should be careful who you show that trick to. It's kind of a show stopper."

"I won my share of bar bets with it, let me tell you." She saw his expression and explained, "In college. When I was less discreet. I haven't tried it in...well, there's been no...umm..."

"No recent tongue-to-tongue demonstrations?"

She ducked her head. "You might say that."

"Want to try?"

Her gaze flew up to collide with his, then away like a frightened bird. For a woman who'd just knotted a cherry stem with her tongue, the reaction was surprising.

She scanned the beach. Deserted. "All right," she said, so seriously he smiled. She propped her chin on her clasped hands, positioned her lips, and closed her eyes.

"Not like that." He eased an arm around her to turn

her onto her back. She went compliantly, even though her hands sprang open and her eyes widened to show the whites. "Relax," he said, smoothing a hand over her abbreviated silky blue dress.

"Relax? Humph. I'm not a—a—mental patient," she sputtered.

"But you are *im*patient."

Deliberately she took a deep breath and let her body go lax on the exhale. "Better, doctor?" she murmured, her lids lowered, her face serene, bathed in the glow of the moon.

It was his pulse that needed calming now.

"This is becoming a production," he said.

She didn't move, but he detected slivers of blue irises watching him through her lashes. "Isn't that where you excel?" she asked without moving her kiss-poised lips.

His reputation had preceded him. Normally that wouldn't matter, but with Cathy, everything was different and new—even a kiss. Saying so would sound as corny as Kansas. She'd think he was feeding her a line.

He cleared his throat. "Seems I'm out of practice."

"Then if I must." She looped her shawl around his neck. It was soft, warm from her body, and he caught a whiff of the scent clinging to it as she pulled him toward herself. His arms trembled with tension as he lowered himself over her body. She licked her lips. And just before he took her mouth, he looked into her eyes and saw the pure emotion that her playfulness had veiled.

Their kiss was a bittersweet blend of wonder and aching need. It was an easy kiss, even though he felt rubbed raw, all that tightly wound desire an abrasive against his nerve endings. Slowly he savored her mouth, tasting her, touching her, suppressing the urge to plunge his tongue deep and make her squirm and moan with passion. She was too fragile in his arms. Her caresses were light and tentative, as if she had to think about each one before bestowing it. As if she'd never done this before.

Well, neither had he.

So this is our beginning, he thought, sliding his mouth from side to side against her soft parted lips with a motion so slow and luxurious it felt like floating. They *were* floating. But not on a hard wooden raft. On a cloud, a feather bed—a silken sun-drenched sea. Moving together in the undulant waves like sea creatures, adrift in the ebb and flow of desire, cradled by one warm gentle kiss after another.

And it was enough. Kissing her was enough, because it felt so good and right and complete—as if they could kiss forever.

Forever without end.

6

"I'M ALWAYS AMAZED that it's so dark and quiet here," Cathy murmured, not to break the silence, but because she needed to move her lips. To break her smile, so to speak. She felt sure it was the goofiest post-kiss smile Zack had ever seen. Nonetheless, she couldn't help it.

She'd never been with a man like Zack, a man who knew the value of long, slow kisses, who didn't immediately pull and grab and press for more. The experience had been a revelation. She was wonderstruck. Still floating on air.

"That's a small town for you." Zack turned the car onto their street. It was cloaked in darkness, shrouded by trees. Most of the houses were closed and silent. All she heard was the smooth purr of the powerful engine and the hum of the tires against the pavement. Way off in the distance a dog barked.

"I'm so glad I chose Quimby." As if he couldn't tell by her expression.

"Why did you?" he asked, parking. He turned the key in the ignition and the silence became complete. Expectant.

"Choose Quimby?" She threaded her fingers through the straps of the sandals in her lap, determined that she would lie to him as little as possible. Tonight especially, after such intimacies, she couldn't bear to be duplicitous.

"My grandparents lived here once." *So did I. Don't you recognize me? Just a little?*

"Who were they? I probably knew them." He left the car.

As he opened her door, she made herself busy retrieving her wrap and the restaurant glass they'd borrowed for the lilies of the valley. "Oh, it was years and years ago. I'm sure you wouldn't remember them. They were old, even then. Not very sociable."

"But you must have visited." He drew her out, his hand sliding to her elbow, trailing pinpricks of scintillation.

"Why do you say that?"

"Obviously you remembered the place well enough to want to return here."

"That was more because it had the right shop for sale." *True. The shop had been the main component to her decision. Of course, the only reason she'd thought to seek her opportunity in Quimby was because of Zack, but she didn't have to go into* that. *Even in the name of honesty.*

Fortunately, he was distracted from further questions. "What's going on here?" he asked as he turned toward the glow of lamplight in the backyard of the Colton bungalow.

"Would you believe fairies?" Cathy said, stepping carefully toward the grass in her bare feet. "Elves?"

He cocked his head at a skeptical angle and thrust his hands into the pockets of his trousers. They were rolled up to his shins, revealing his own bare feet. "An elf named Allie Spangler, maybe."

"We might as well take a look."

The Heartbroken quintet had worked wonders with the seedy backyard. Paper Japanese lanterns had been strung from tree to tree. They glowed like the full moons of an alien planet—yellow, pink, orange, lime. Two Adirondack chairs and a low table were positioned nearby. Cathy squinted. On the table was an ice bucket and bottle, two champagne glasses and a radio-CD player. She added the glassful of lilies.

"I hope they're gone," Zack said, "these nosy elves of yours."

She scanned the windows, also hoping. When the rhododendron bush rustled softly, she half expected Allie to pop out and do a hobbit-like song and dance.

"What's going on?"

Cathy turned to Zack, dropping her sandals in the grass.

"Why the big push?" he said.

"They—uh, I guess they thought I needed a little help in the romancing department."

His expression was quizzical. "Have they *met* you?" he said with such incredulity she blushed. He had no idea what a compliment that was!

She smoothed the periwinkle dress from Laurel's shop. Even though he was aware of his old girlfriends' involvement, clearly he didn't know everything. Learning that his ex-fiancée's hand was stirring the pot would tip the scales from matchmaking to Machiavelli.

"I don't always look like this, Zack." Nervously Cathy ran her fingers through her hair, which had begun slipping out of the chignon. "In fact, I never do. I usually wear flats, glasses and loose dresses. I'm not—"

Suddenly he was right in front of her, searching her eyes. She blinked myopically. Let him see only her sincerity. Not her tangled motives.

"Do you think I care what clothes you wear?"

He sounded so fervent, she believed every word.

Twenty years hadn't changed him. He'd always looked beyond the surface. The engagement to Laurel was an aberration. It had to be.

Please, oh, please, she thought. *Let Zack Brody be all the man I've built him up to be.*

When he smiled and put his hand out to her, she went to him with her heart so full of hope and joy that the whys and wherefores of their union—or reunion—no longer mattered.

"AW, ISN'T THAT SWEET?" Julia said from behind the wheel of a handsome town car parked at the curb. They had an oblique view into the romantically illuminated backyard.

Laurel's stare was smoldering. "Not sweet." Her top lip lifted. "Saccharine."

Except for Allie, they'd been hunkered down at Gwen's house two streets away for the past half hour, watching for the return of Zack's Jag. Earlier, Laurel had called Jerome's to check on the progress of dinner only to learn that their big fish had slipped the net. She'd been in a sour mood ever since.

"Boy," Gwen said from the back seat. "The plan's really working."

"Appears to be," Julia murmured.

Music played, accompanied by a smoky, throaty crooning that went perfectly with the warm early summer night. Zack and Cathy danced barefoot in the grass, cheek-to-cheek, clinging like limpets. One of his hands was pressed to the hollow of her back. The other clasped hers down low, at their hips. Now and then he turned his head and raised her hand, kissing the back of it with a tenderness that was as clear as day to each and every one of their observers.

It was a scene guaranteed to make a woman—any woman—get all mushy and sentimental. And to make a man think he was gonna get some.

"What do you think, Faith?" Julia turned to look into the back seat. "Fai—"

Faith was mesmerized. Her eyes were glazed, her fingers knotted beneath her chin. Her mouth hung open, steaming up the car window.

"Faith's gone bye-bye," Gwen said. "Faith's in another world." She gave the secretary a shove. "Wake up from the dream, girl. Heartbreak's passed you by again."

"Wha—" Faith jerked around, blushing furiously. For an instant she looked angry, but then she cast her gaze into her lap and mumbled unintelligibly. "Brmmph..."

Julia was contemplative. "Perhaps our plan is working too well."

"How reliable is Cathy?" Laurel's eyes narrowed. "We don't really know that much about her, do we? She's very quiet. Why, she could be double-crossing us right this moment!"

"Aw, she's too meek for that."

"I know her well enough," Julia said. "The worry should be that Zack is going to work his usual magic on her. Look." She waved toward the scene in the backyard. "What woman could resist?"

"We'll just have to set her straight."

"How do you propose we do that, Laurel?"

"By telling her a few harsh truths about that sneaking, cowardly ex-fiancé of mine!"

"You've already done a fine job of besmirching Zack's reputation. All around town."

"I've every right." Laurel aimed a cutting look at Julia. "It wasn't *you* left standing at the altar."

"I know," she said with a tired sigh.

"And for that, Zack must suffer." Laurel leaned toward her open window. "Ahhh. Here we go." There was a short silence before the next song began with a catchy beat and a mellow sax. "Listen to this—Zack's theme song."

Gwen smirked when she recognized the lyrics. "That'll give Cath a jolt of reality."

Julia cocked her head. "Hmm...it's a clever jab. I didn't know you could be so *subtle*, Laurel."

Faith listened with her eyes closed and her hands pressed to her cheeks, hiding most of her face.

The jazzy strains of music carried across the dark lawn, weaving a seductive spell from lyrics of deceit and treachery. But the swaying couple didn't seem to notice. They kept dancing, heads together, eyes closed. Blissfully oblivious to Laurel's little ploy.

The song was Sade's "Smooth Operator."

THE NEXT MORNING, Cathy's telephone woke her up. *Brrrrp. Brrrrp. Brrrrp.* Bleary-eyed, she blinked at the alarm clock beside the bed. Seven something. Let the machine pick up. She pulled a pillow over her head and went back to sleep.

Minutes later, she woke with a start. The phone was ringing again. The upstairs extension was on the floor beside her bed, but she didn't reach for it. Zack wouldn't call so early, so it had to be one of the Heartbroken gang. Definitely let the machine pick up, she said to herself and rolled to the far side of the bed.

The phone continued to shrill at fifteen-minute intervals. Annoyance forced her out of bed and into the shower. She hadn't figured out how to explain the evening to her puppeteers. But she sure couldn't think with that darn phone drilling into her skull.

Cathy dressed and went downstairs, purposely focusing on the kite-high optimism that lingered from the past night. She looked around her with a sense of wonder. The house hadn't changed. Despite her attempts to refurbish it with fresh paint, sari-fabric curtains and bright Georgia O'Keefe flower prints, it remained a humble cottage, worn from years of the Colton family's abuse. Yet this morning everything looked good to her.

Knowing why, smiling self-consciously, she rubbed the initials carved into the newel post. *A.C.* + *Z.B.*

She traced her own initials over the *A.C.* At age ten, she'd inscribed Zack's name on the cover of her school notebook and then hurriedly blacked it out, afraid someone would see and make fun of her crush on the most popular boy in the fifth grade. Bad enough that they'd called her Cathy Beachball or Cathy Big Belly whenever Zack wasn't around to make them stop. If he'd found out from their classmates that she "lo-o-o-oved" him, the poor kid would have really been put on the spot. Even Zack's kindness could extend only so far.

Cathy stepped into the living room, her outlook dimming. Had things changed, really? Already she and Zack had formed a tight but separate friendship. Outside forces worked to pull them apart. The difference was that this time, it was she who'd be subjected to peer pressure. The Heartbroken wanted Zack to feel the pain of being a social outcast. She was to be the instrument of his destruction.

Cathy didn't have it in her to be mean to a fly. The Admiral used to tell her to toughen up, but the most she'd ever managed was a brittle protective shell. Inside she was as soft and empathetic—and as easily hurt—as ever.

The sudden, high-pitched ring of the phone made her jump. She did not want to talk to any of the Wednesday nighters, except perhaps for Julia.

The message clicked on. *"Hello, this is Cathy Timmerman's answering machine..."*

After the beep, Zack's voice came over the speaker. "Cathy? Sorry, I know it's early, but I had this idea—"

Lightning quick, she snatched up the receiver. "Zack? Good morning! I didn't know it was you who kept calling or I'd have...oh, you didn't?" Not him, he said, mentioning a busy tone, calling her Miss Popular. Her answering laugh was hollow with irony, but he didn't notice. She agreed to meet him outside in five minutes—forgetting how forcefully Laurel had drilled her on the necessity of playing hard-to-get—then hung up to check her messages.

Gwen, first: "Holy commotion, Cathy! What happened last night? Call me right away!"

Then Laurel, her ladylike tone underlined with acid: "Laurel Barnard here. We saw you two dancing. I hope you aren't thinking you'll succeed where all else have failed. That wouldn't do."

Gwen again: "Cath? Cath? Aren'tcha up yet?"

Allie, yawning: "Jeesh, did I get an earful from Gwen last night about your date with Zack. Sounds like you worked wonders." A long silence. "So call me. I want to know every gory detail."

Laurel, clipped: "I'm leaving for church, but we're going to meet this afternoon. All of us. We've decided you need a refresher course on the dos and don'ts of dating Zack."

Julia: "Cathy, this is Julia. I'm afraid Laurel and some of the others have worked themselves into a tizzy. It seems you appeared to be a tad too successful with

MILLS & BOON®

An Important Message from The Editors of Mills & Boon®

Dear Reader,

Because you've chosen to read one of our romance novels, we'd like to say "thank you"!

And, as a **special way** to thank you, we've selected <u>two more</u> of the <u>books</u> you love so much **and** a welcome gift to send you absolutely <u>FREE</u>!

Please enjoy them with our compliments...

Tessa Shapcott

Editor, Mills & Boon

P.S. And because we value our customers we've attached something extra inside...

EDITOR'S "THANK YOU" SEAL

PEEL OFF AND PLACE INSIDE

How to validate your Editor's Free Gift "Thank You"

1. **Peel off the Free Gift Seal** from the front cover. Place it in the space provided to the right. This automatically entitles you to receive two free books and a beautiful gold-plated Austrian crystal necklace.

2. **Complete your details** on the card, detach along the dotted line, and post it back to us. No stamp needed. We'll then send you two free novels from the Sensual Romance™ series. These books have a retail value of £2.55, but are yours to keep absolutely free.

3. **Enjoy the read.** We hope that after receiving your free books you'll want to remain a subscriber. But the choice is yours - to continue or cancel, any time at all! So why not accept our no risk invitation? You'll be glad you did.

Your satisfaction is guaranteed

You're under no obligation to buy anything. We charge you nothing for your introductory parcel. And you don't have to make any minimum number of purchases – not even one! Thousands of readers have already discovered that the Reader Service™ is the most convenient way of enjoying the latest new romance novels before they are available in the shops. Of course, postage and packing to your home is completely FREE.

Tessa Shapcott

Editor, Mills & Boon

The Editor's "Thank You"

You'll love this exquisite gold-plated necklace with its 46cm (18") cobra linked chain and multi-faceted Austrian crystal which sparkles just like a diamond. It's the perfect accessory to dress up any outfit, casual or formal. RESPOND TODAY AND IT'S YOURS FREE.

Not actual size

◄ **Detach along the dotted line and post this card today. No Stamp Needed** ►

Yes! Please send me my two FREE books and a welcome gift

PLACE EDITOR'S "THANK YOU" SEAL HERE

Yes! I have placed my free gift seal in the space provided above. Please send me my two free books along with my welcome gift. I understand I am under no obligation to purchase any books, as explained on the back and opposite page. I am over 18 years of age.

T2EI

BLOCK CAPITALS

Surname (Mrs/Ms/Miss/Mr) _____ Initials_____

Address _____

_____

_____

_____ Postcode _____

► **Detach and keep your complimentary book mark.** ►

The Reader Service™

FREEPOST CN81

CROYDON

CR9 3WZ

NO
STAMP
NEEDED

If this offer card is missing, please write to: The Reader Service, P.O. Box 236, Croydon, CR9 3RU

Zack. Heads shall roll." She laughed. "Oh, well. I hope you had a good time. It looked like you did. Call me, we'll talk—figure something out. Bye."

Allie, voice raised to compete with background noise: "Is it true? Have you fallen for Zack? I know he's hard to resist, but, cripes, girl, couldn't you hold out—*Brendan, stop writing on your sister right this min*—" Click.

Beeeep.

Cathy blinked. They already knew—or were reasonably sure—that she'd fallen for Zack? Was it that obvious?

What about Zack?

She shivered, even though it had to be eighty outside. What *about* Zack? He was waiting for her. Should she go with him, or wait for the Heartbroken to descend en masse?

No choice.

Cathy spilled the contents of her evening purse on the coffee table, fished out a lipstick, a small stash of cash and her driver's license. She stuffed them into the front pocket of her cutoffs, changed her glasses for a pair of prescription shades and headed out the door.

What the Heartbroken didn't know wouldn't make them jealous.

"MMM, THIS IS GOOD," Cathy said as she poured another dollop of pure maple syrup on a half-devoured stack of apple pancakes. "You really know how to feed a girl, Zack."

"Bacon?"

She glanced at the plate he offered. "I shouldn't." She weighed a forkful of dripping pancake, then popped the entire bite into her mouth. "Mmmph. Okay. Bring it on."

He tipped three slices onto her plate. "I like a female who knows how to eat."

Cathy stopped chewing. She stabbed her fork into the stack and left it there. "That's not particularly a compliment, you know," she said after she'd swallowed thickly. "I'm usually pretty stringent about watching what I eat."

"Oh, sure, sure," he said, nodding and cutting into his own pile of buckwheat cakes. "And it shows." He glanced at her clingy little red tank top, and the curves it revealed more than concealed. Its brevity also provided him with two inches of tanned, toned midriff for inspection. No—for admiration. "It shows very nicely."

She glowered at the pancakes. "I used to have a weight problem."

"No." He couldn't believe it. "What are we talking, a pesky five extra pounds, right?"

"Try fifty." She licked her fork calmly enough, but he could tell by the gravity in her voice that she was uncomfortable. Especially when she ducked her head, pretending that scrubbing at her sticky fingers with a paper napkin was of tantamount importance.

He squinted at her. "I can't quite picture it."

She repositioned the sunglasses she'd pushed to the top of her head, tucking her hair behind her ears. "Don't try too hard."

"I'll bet you were round and voluptuous."

Her lips compressed.

"Sweet and juicy as a ripe peach."

They twitched at the corners.

"You were probably worthy of one of the great artists of the Renaissance. You'd have made a gorgeous, sumptuous nude masterpiece."

"Dream on."

"Think I will." He leaned back in the comfortable old leatherette booth of the roadside diner, closed his eyes and gave a deep sigh. "Hmm. Cathy Timmerman, lounging nude among the velvet robes and brocade tapestries. Um-hummm..." He watched her reaction through slitted eyelids.

Even though she tried to look exasperated, there was something pleased and flattered about her expression. She was still battling her smile. "Gimme a break."

"Cathy Timmerman. Naked odalisque..."

"Stop that." She sawed at her pancakes. "Right now." Concentrating, she stabbed the tines of her fork—already loaded with four triangles of pancake—through a pink curl of bacon and lifted the entire construction to her mouth. "This is an inappropriate conversation for Sunday morning breakfast."

Which sounded like something his mother used to say whenever the three males of the family became the least bit raunchy. He leaned closer to the table, eyeing Cathy over the syrup bottles and juice glasses. "Are you a prude?" he asked, thinking, *Heck, no.* She and his mother would get along—they were both modest, but not inhibited. He remembered how his parents used to kiss in the kitchen when they were doing dishes.

Cathy tilted her chin. "I am reserved."

"Reserved? I like that."

She looked doubtful.

He winked. "Reserved for me."

She seemed to be holding her breath. Her eyes bulged. Tension ballooned between them until finally she let out a sharp pinprick of a giggle. "Like a library book, huh?"

He worked his eyebrows up and down. "Something tells me I'll be paying overdue fines."

She put down her fork to sputter into a napkin.

"So why'd you lose the weight?" he said when she was under control.

"Don't you mean *how?*"

"No."

"Oh." She frowned. "What world are you living in that you could even ask that question?"

He shrugged. "I just happen to think you'd look fine either way."

"Dated lots of fat girls, have you?"

He paused. "A few who were...plump. Curves are nice. In fact, curves are one of the things I look for in a woman."

She poked at the sodden pancakes, brooding. "Oh, sorry. I forgot. You're Heartbreak Brody. Come one, come all. Every make and model. All shapes, sizes, colors and personalities."

"I've never gone out with a woman I didn't respect."

"An equal opportunity player."

"You might say that. But I don't."

Cathy looked out the speckled window at the gravel parking lot rimmed with weeds. A logging truck rumbled past on Highway 452. "I'm trying to decide if that explains Laurel Barnard."

He recoiled, feeling as if she'd twisted a knife in his gut. "I wouldn't call what Laurel and I did dating."

Suspicion and curiosity warred in Cathy's sky-blue eyes. Her mouth pulled taut. "Want to explain that?" *Can you?* she seemed to imply, drumming her fingertips on the table.

"I can tell you some of it," he said. "But the rest will have to wait until I've spoken to Laurel."

"A gentleman to the end." Her voice had softened, though her eyes still regarded him narrowly. He supposed she had reason to doubt his good intentions.

"Let's get out of here," he said, suddenly choked by the thick greasy air. The checked linoleum was dingy and cracked. A fly bumbled against a windowpane washed in harsh sunlight.

Cathy slid out of the booth. He threw a twenty on the table, eager to leave. But on the way out, he spotted a familiar face at the counter, one hard to pass by. He stopped to offer his hand. "Reggie Lee. Good to see you, buddy."

Reggie Lee exclaimed and pumped Zack's hand.

Zack touched Cathy's shoulder, but she was already turning to greet the handyman like a longtime friend. "Then we all know each other?" Zack said. "No introductions necessary?"

Reggie Lee tugged on his cap. "I done some work for Mrs. Timmerman at her store."

"You've been taking care of my yard, too. Doing a nice job of it."

"Miss Julia hired me regular. I do five yards for her now—youse two on Curran street, two on Brinkner Avenue and one out on Quarry Road. That's a big 'un."

"It's good to keep busy," Cathy said.

"Sure is, ma'am. After them Barnards fired me, it was Miss Julia said I should come work for her. She saved my bacon, my mom says, 'cause, y'know..." Reggie Lee somehow managed to smile, nod and shrug all at once.

Zack was taken aback. "Leo Barnard fired you?"

"Well, yessir. Right after the wedding. I mean, after the, uh, the—" Reggie Lee lowered his voice. "*The trouble.*" His eyes shifted. "They didn't want me sayin' nothin'."

Zack could say nothing, either.

"My mom says don't spread no gossip, not even 'bout the letter. So I kept my mouth shut."

It was Cathy who broke the ensuing silence. "Quite right, Reggie Lee. You're a good man."

Zack cleared his throat, arranged to have the handyman continue mowing his lawn, then made his goodbyes and escorted Cathy out of the diner before they could run into another helpful and talkative Quimbyite. Their conversation at breakfast had already taken a turn toward a complicated and dangerous territory. Now he could literally feel the curiosity she radiated.

He couldn't blame her. Many of the locals seemed to hold him entirely responsible for the cancelled wedding. Naturally Cathy would have picked up on the feeling.

"What now?" she said, lowering her sunglasses. She left her hands knitted on top of her head, which slid the edge of her top up another two inches. Her stomach was flat, but the arch of her rib cage made it into a smooth rounded oval, indented by her navel like a dimple in a dish of cream. The loose, unbelted waistband of her denim shorts hung low on her hips. Suddenly he wanted to slide his hand along her belly, dip low past her waistband, then up beneath her skimpy little top to test the weight of her breasts.

He looked away. Cathy would run if she knew what he'd been thinking. She wasn't the type of woman eager to be groped by a man with as shady a reputation as his seemed to be these days. So he was going to have to settle his scores. Real soon. Because groping Cathy Timmerman was definitely on his agenda.

"Feel like getting some exercise?" he said, still not looking at her. He shadowed his eyes with his palm. The day was turning hot and humid. There was a quarry pond just up the hill, but they'd have to walk a mile through the woods to reach it.

She didn't hesitate. It was possible he'd overestimated

her reaction to his bad reputation. "I have to work off that breakfast, don't I?"

He took her hand. "Then let's go."

There were fews things as gripping as the first glimpse of blue water through a dense forest. A hot, buggy, dense, leafy forest, Cathy thought. She brushed her arm across her sweaty face. "I see blue. Is that it?"

"Nearly there," Zack said, bushwhacking in front of her.

"Thank heaven."

"Sorry about this." He held up a thick branch laden with pine cones so she could pass beneath it. "It's been a number of years since I was here. The trail has grown in a lot since then."

"Trail? Where I come from, we call vegetation like this a jungle."

"No cobras here," he said, just as something cool and slithery touched her leg. She yelped and crashed through the last several yards of the fern-choked path, then stopped abruptly where the trees gave way to long grass and slabs of dusky red rock. Sunshine danced upon the surface of the pond, so shockingly bright and electric she pulled out her sunglasses to cut the glare.

Zack came up behind her and slid his hands along her arms. His touch was distracting, and he'd been touching her a lot. Holding her hand, wiping her perspiring face with his bandanna, kissing her—on her cheek, her hand, her shoulder, even the back of her knee when she thought she'd been stung by a wasp. The wasp had turned out to be a noseeum. Which was fortunate because his touch had excited her more than it had soothed her.

"It's nice, isn't it?"

She leaned against him, shimmying her shoulders into the hot broad wall of his chest, and purred, "*Very* nice."

His head lowered. "I meant the quarry pond." His tongue flicked her lobe.

"Why isn't anyone else here?"

"Don't know. Maybe the kids today are too lazy to make the walk. Heck, when I was a boy—"

"Grandpa," she joshed.

He squeezed her. "When I was a young whippersnapper, my friends and I split our summer between the quarry pond and Mirror Lake. The quarry was more fun, but the public beach had girls."

Cathy moved away before he could feel her muscles tense up. During her year in Quimby, she'd gone to the public beach exactly once—and come home with the name Cathy Beachball. The remainder of her tenth summer had been spent in her grandparents' screened porch, cutting paper dolls and eating Suzy Qs.

But I am different now, she vowed. She perched boldly at the lip of a rock ledge that jutted out over the rippling water and removed her sunglasses. "Are we skinny-dipping?" That should shock him. And prove to herself that she wasn't Cathy Beachball anymore.

"I can't guarantee privacy, but sure." Zack tore off his shirt. "Let's skinny-dip."

Of course he'd say that. Regardless of his discretion up to now, he was still a man. All the way through.

She got as far as stepping out of her shoes and shorts before chickening out. "Um, I think I'll retain my modesty."

"Spoilsport." Zack joined her on the edge, wearing only his khaki shorts and the twisted bandanna knotted loosely around his neck. His hair was rumpled, his eyes were gleeful and his chest was a work of art worthy of

Michelangelo except for a sheen of perspiration that glistened in the sunshine and made him very, very real. His masculine scent tickled her nostrils—provocative as heck.

"This—" she gestured at her stretchy red tank top and burgundy Jockey bikini briefs "—is practically a bathing suit. A tankini, it's called."

"Not eenie enough, but tank you anyway."

She laughed and gave Zack a shove, thinking she could push him off the rock. Ha! His chest was as solid as a slab of beef.

"Want to get thrown in?" he said. "Because I'm the man for the job."

She peered over the edge. The drop was long. The water turned a darker blue close to the rocks. It looked deep and cold. "Too far for me," she said. "Is the water cold?"

"Not too cold. See that flat pink rock? You can climb down and jump from there. It's safe."

In no time, she'd scuttled along the smooth, cut slabs to the lower level. The jump was nominal—but still she hesitated.

"Go on," Zack encouraged.

Here's to Cathy Beachball. She took a few running steps and leapt as far as possible out over the water, limbs spreadeagled like a skydiver so she'd make a huge splash.

She did, but she didn't notice. The shock of the cold water drove everything else out of her mind. She shot up to the surface, exclamations exploding off her lips. "Gah! That's cold!"

Zack peered at her from above, his hands on his knees. "Are you okay?"

She flailed at the water, as if she could push its frigid embrace away from herself. "You lied!"

"It's not *too* cold."

She sputtered, her breath coming in shuddering gasps. "Then why—don't you—jump?"

He stood poised on the granite ledge, arms outspread, silhouetted against the stark blue and white of the sky. She forgot the cold as he went up on the balls of his feet, raising his arms overhead, making himself into an arrow of taut muscle and bone.

And then he dove, touching his toes in a perfect jack-knife before straightening to cut into the water with a physical assurance that was breathtaking. There was barely a ripple to mark his entry.

Cathy's heart clenched. Zack Brody was the essence of masculine beauty.

And *she* was supposed to seduce *him?*

The setup was laughable. Cathy Beachball versus a suntanned sex god.

He surfaced toward the middle of the pond. They swam toward each other through the cold clean water. She was awestruck, her inner voice babbling like a teenybopper meeting a boy band.

She stopped, blinking at him while she tread the icy water. Her teeth chattered when her mouth was closed, so she opened it. And said, of all things, "Got shrink-age?"

Zack's expression was memorable.

He spat out a mouthful of water. "Wha-what?"

She bared her chattering teeth. "The water's cold, isn't it?" She turned to swim away. "But not *too* cold, I hope. Considering."

"You minx," he said, making a lunge at her. He snagged her ankle, dragged her beneath the surface. She fought against him, even though her hopes were buoyed by close contact with his shoulders and chest. They were both laughing when they surfaced.

They played like kids for a few minutes, splashing, diving, shouting with high spirits. She climbed aboard his shoulders and he lifted her out of the water toward the blessed hot sun for one glorious instant before he flipped her off backward and again she plunged into the cold blue depths.

Finally they'd had enough. They raced to the rocks, Cathy huffing and puffing as she fell far behind Zack, who glided through the water like a dolphin, if a dolphin had broad brown shoulders. He was magnificent to watch, and she forgot again about the plot against him and the race and even the cold until he touched the rock and turned to look for her, his teeth flashing white in the sun.

She paddled to his side. "Mr. Swim Team," she said, hoisting herself half out of the water onto the slanted slab of wet red rock.

He slapped her behind in a friendly way. "What do I win?"

She collapsed against the stone, flabbergasted that her body could flush with heat even when it shuddered with cold. Friendly or not, Zack's handprint burned right through her thin wet panties and into her flesh. Her pulse picked up. Every touch was better than the last, but the effect was cumulative, making her fizzle with reaction—a chemistry experiment foaming from a beaker. Hot froth. Pure sensation.

"You win this," she said breathlessly, dipping her foot into the water with the intention of splashing his face. He gripped her calf and gave her leg a tug. She slid off the slick slanted rock and landed—*splash*—in the pond.

"I win this," he said, and kissed her.

Smooth Moves

His lips were cold. His mouth was warm. And she...she was drowning all over again.

"Solved your shrinkage problem?" she said, gasping for breath.

He nipped her lobe. "Another kiss ought to do it."

"Then it's time to stop." She reached for a good grip on the rock and surged up out of the water. "I'm a sweet innocent. I can't handle all this hot and heavy action."

"No worry." He ran a hand through his slicked-back hair, staring intently as she scrambled up onto all fours, then looked around at him. His pupils had closed to ebony pinpoints. "I can."

"Yeah. That's what I'm afraid of." She risked another quick glance, then clambered over the rocks till she reached the top, her heart pounding as if she'd reached the summit of Everest. Zack joined her a minute later and she turned to him with her arms crossed over her breasts. "Now what do we do?"

"We bake on the rocks."

He was too polite to leer at her suddenly much too thin and clingy undies and tank, but she did see his eyes darken as his gaze slipped across her. She clutched her biceps. *You are a seductress*, she told herself. Nevertheless, it took all her willpower to drop her arms and walk calmly to a large flat rock, to turn and spread herself across it as though she hadn't a modest bone in her body.

And he didn't have an immodest boner in his shorts.

Ye gods! Her lids slammed shut.

She'd counted three hundred and forty-six non-shrinkage seconds before Zack came to lay down beside her. The rock was immense—there was plenty of room for both of them, even with their limbs spread. She peeked through her spiky lashes, moving her hand ever so slightly till their fingertips brushed. He wasn't as shy. His fingers twined through hers and the simple, uncomplicated contact filled her with happiness.

The rock was smooth and warm beneath her, the sun blazing above. She sighed, trying not to think about their kiss and of course thinking of nothing else. "Ahhh," she said, resorting to cliché. "This is the life."

"Mm-hmm."

"Why'd you ever leave?" It was a good, neutral subject, and she started to relax.

"Career," he said lazily.

"But that's changed?"

"I took a leave of absence to go to Idaho. Recently, though, I turned in my resignation."

The insides of her eyelids were orange. "I didn't know that. Do you have plans, then?"

He made an amused sound. "No five-year plan, but I've decided to stay in Quimby. I'll be the only architect for a hundred miles, so I might even be able to make a living."

"Um." Cathy's thoughts drifted. A faint buzzing—the insect world's constant chorus—filled the air. "What'll Laurel say?" she asked after a while, barely moving her lips. She could *feel* her hair drying.

Zack sighed. "Laurel again."

"We have to talk about her sometime." Cathy rolled her head against the stone, scraping damp hair from her nape. "I hear the breakup was rather sudden." *A bald understatement.*

"The situation was complicated." His grip tightened, then released. Her palm was sweaty. "But the end was quick and clean."

"Quick, yes. But clean? I don't think so."

"The mess was mostly Laurel's making," he insisted.

Cathy bolted upright. "You were her fiancé!"

"By default," he said.

"I don't understand..."

"She was pregnant, Cathy."

"Oh."

Zack's eyes were closed; his face was hard. "I doubted her at first. But she showed me the test results and they looked authentic. I had no choice—the baby deserved a name."

Cathy's brain buzzed with questions. "But there is no baby."

"A miscarriage, she claimed. Two weeks before the wedding." He sat up slowly and passed his hand over his face. His eyes were slitted against the sunshine. "I don't know. It might have been true. She did go to the hospital, but I only found out afterward."

"Then that—there no longer being a baby—was why you cancelled the wedding?"

"Not entirely. Laurel was in hysterics—she'd planned this gala of a wedding, an incredible feat in such a short time. She pleaded with me not to back out. Said I couldn't humiliate her that way. I felt it was the honorable thing to follow through...." He shook his head. "Even though I knew the marriage wouldn't last."

"You weren't—" Cathy's voice caught in her throat. "You weren't in love with her?" But he'd been willing to get her pregnant. The reality of that altered her perception of him, wrenching at her emotions until she was bleak and drained. Even the saturated colors of the sky and the trees and the deep blue water had faded like an old photograph.

He sounded bitter. "I was never in love with Laurel Barnard. She knew it and she did not care. I was a good name to her, a prime catch. A suit to prop up at the altar and say *I do*."

They sat in silence, Zack's final words as hard and jarring as the bleached, sliced-stone landscape. The thick branches of the towering evergreens hung heavy and still in the hot summer haze.

"Still..." Cathy said tentatively.

He turned his head. "It's more complicated than you know. Than I can tell you. My brother had left town on bad terms. A day before the wedding I got word that he'd been in a serious car wreck. He's my family—I had to go. Before I left, I tried to talk to Laurel. She—" He stopped to heave a tired sigh. "She had time to cancel the wedding."

Cathy frowned. There was more to the story—the part he'd said he wouldn't tell. He couldn't have intended for Laurel to stand alone at the altar and send the guests home. But how—why—? Everyone in town believed he'd jilted her.

A crow cawed in the distance, and Cathy realized that she didn't want to talk about this any longer. It was all too harsh and painful.

She softened her voice. "What happened with your brother?"

Zack breathed deeply. "At first the doctors thought he'd never walk again. Adam's a fighter, though. He's still taking physical therapy and the progress has been slow, but he's walking better every day."

"That's good."

"It's very good."

She drew her knees up to her chin. "Wow. Living in Quimby is kind of like finding myself cast in a soap opera."

He offered up a weak imitation of his usual devastating smile. "Can we keep this between us? Allie, Julia, *Gwen*—they don't know about Laurel's pregnancy."

"I won't speak of it. Although there must have been rumors."

"Sure. But you know Laurel. She had a perfect wedding in mind—she couldn't stand the thought of everyone gossiping behind her back."

"I guess." Cathy laid one hand flat against the red granite and studied the jagged pattern of her outspread fingers. He'd risked his own reputation to protect Laurel. He was still protecting her. Did he have residual feelings for the woman? Why not? Laurel had nearly become his bride.

Cathy thought of the bitterness in his voice and decided that whatever they were, his feelings weren't romantic. But there was a thin line between love and hate.

She brushed her fingers over the rough stone, hopelessly snarled in the complicated web they'd woven. His past. Her secret.

Their future.

If they had one.

7

CATHY KNEW what was coming. She thought she was prepared for it.

Ten minutes after she'd opened up shop Monday morning, Laurel Barnard arrived like a thunderclap. "Cathy!" she shouted, briskly searching the shop. She stopped at the worktable and all but stamped her foot, her green eyes snapping with petulance. "Didn't you get my messages? And Allie's, and Gwen's, and—"

"Sorry." Cathy hoped that one word would suffice. She was not sorry for missing Laurel's "meeting." But she was guilty of purposely avoiding the group. "I didn't listen to all the messages—" *a fine case of semantics* "—until late last night." After it was too late to call anyone back.

Laurel stabbed her hands onto her hips, wrinkling her sarong-style skirt. "Where were you all day? Allie and I stopped at your house."

"Oh, out and about." With Zack, which was what Laurel really wanted to know, but Cathy wasn't telling. By mutual unspoken accord, she and Zack had kept the conversation light after leaving the quarry pond. They'd spent the rest of the day together, driving around the countryside, buying too many fresh fruits and vegetables at a farmer's roadside stand, scouting out the video store and talking movies for close to an hour. Come nightfall, they'd holed up at Zack's place for fruit salad and an encore showing of a mutual favorite, *Zero Effect*.

With a suspicious air, Laurel looked her over. "You're sunburned."

Cathy touched her nose. It was slightly red. "That's summer for you."

"Let me guess. Zack took you swimming. He does that with everyone, you know. It's so predictable."

It was an effort for Cathy to stay nonchalant when her insides were churning. "In that case, I'm surprised you didn't think to look for us at the beach."

Laurel smoothed her skirt. "I don't go after men. They come after me."

"Then why in hell don't you leave Zack alone?" Cathy said, surprising herself with her sudden vehemence... but positively shocking Laurel.

"Because our score is not settled," Laurel spat, with all the venom of a poisonous snake. She leveled a pointed finger at Cathy's face. "Don't even think of trying to hook up until I'm finished with him. *Then* you can have him, for all I care."

Cathy was shaken, but she did not show it. Calmly she continued sorting floss for the Monday night embroidery class, refusing Laurel the biting verbal response that could lead to a screeching match. All this fussing and conniving over a man was starting to seem so juvenile. She wanted no part of it—

Which wasn't strictly true. She did want a part of it— she wanted Zack. But not at any cost.

The trick would be in the withdrawal. Maybe after yesterday, Laurel had already given up on her as an inadequate pawn. Which would be a blessing, Cathy now saw. *Please give me the ax, Laurel. Save me the grief.*

But Laurel had turned on her heel and was marching

away. "Stick to the plan, Cathy." With a flick of her chestnut hair, she threw a grimly satisfied look over her shoulder. "Besides, if you think about it, you'll see that it's much too late to back out." The door swung shut behind her.

Cathy slid into one of her hand-painted chairs. Of course. If she tried to put a halt to the seduction ploy, Laurel would tell Zack everything—that Cathy was a fake, that it was all a setup. And she'd come off looking as phony and manipulative as Laurel herself.

Doesn't matter. Even so, Cathy felt sick. *Zack will understand once he learns who I really am.*

Total confession. She'd have to admit to being Cathy Beachball.

Was that so awful?

Frankly, yes.

She could already imagine the shock, the guffaws... the scorn. Even the oozy sympathy and friendship that could be as much a trial to bear.

Nevertheless, she'd do it for Zack. Once she was one hundred percent sure that he was worth it. As close as they'd become, she was practical enough to remember that it had been only a few days. No way was she ready to risk exposure of her vulnerabilities when she might yet learn that their relationship was little more than another of his playboy games. She was too inexperienced to recognize a player when she kissed one. Look how bad her judgment had been regarding Chad.

The doorbell chimed. Cathy walked toward the front of the store, arms crossed defensively over her work apron. Another of the Heartbroken? She'd have to say "No, thank you, Laurel has already ruined my morning."

It was Julia, dressed in a lightweight beige suit and

carrying two coffees. "Yours is full-strength cappuccino," she said. "Figured you could use the extra zap of caffeine. I saw Laurel as she was leaving."

"Thanks. You're an angel." Cathy peeled off the cover, inhaled the pungent steam as it fogged her glasses, then took a tentative sip. Strong, sweet, milky. "I'm in trouble," she blurted.

"I know." Julia's gaze was steady beneath the bangs that framed her face. "But as aggravating as Laurel can be, it's what's happening between you and Zack that concerns me."

"Me, too," Cathy said, then caught herself. She hesitated, licking foam off her lip, unwilling to meet Julia's frank stare. "How do you know there's something going on between me and Zack?"

"I succumbed to the Brody charm, too, remember? I'm wise to his ways."

Cathy blinked behind her defogged lenses. Of course. Julia would know if he was serious or if his actions were par for the course. Julia could tell her what to do.

"Do you have time to talk? Want to go in the back with me while I unpack cartons?"

Julia shrugged. "I have nothing but time. There's not much action on the Quimby real estate market lately. I've sold every property that's even remotely saleable and now I'm starting on reselling them."

"Zack might be looking."

Julia's brows arched. "Not for a house, surely. I always doubted he'd actually follow through with the sale of his family home, even if he did say to put it on the market."

Cathy left the door to the cluttered storage room open so she could hear the bell. She swept a stack of feather packets off a chair and offered it to Julia. "Then you never really put his house up for sale while he was gone? That was thoughtful."

"Oh, I stuck a sign in the yard. Even showed the occasional client through the house." Julia's top lip curved around the rim of the coffee cup. "But I made certain to mention the faulty wiring and the risk of flooding from the river. In the interest of full disclosure, of course."

Cathy smiled. "You were positive he'd come back."

"Yes. A bunch of gossipmongers and a little whiff of scandal wouldn't keep Zack away permanently. In fact, that was what always confounded me about him jilting Laurel. I'd have expected Zack to deal with the matter head-on." Julia plucked a tiny feather off her skirt and studied it broodingly. "It's Adam who's the 'eat my dust' type." She blew the feather into the air, then caught it in her palm.

While Cathy unpacked a shipment of doll's body parts, Julia played with the tiny feather and went on to relate a story illuminating Zack's tendency to stand tough and take responsibility for misdeeds that were likely the fault of Allie and Adam. Cathy was calculating whether the emotion in her friend's voice was regret or nostalgia. Up to now, Julia had seemed the most equable regarding her breakup with Zack. Why did telling of the time Allie and Adam set fire to Zack's favorite Lincoln-Log construction put a catch in her throat?

"Well, Zack claims he's back to stay," Cathy said once Julia had wound down. "He wants to set up shop as an architect."

"That's a surprise. He used to joke that he wouldn't come back to Quimby until he'd built the eighth wonder of the world." Julia's gaze lingered on Cathy. "Hmm. I wonder what changed his mind?"

Cathy stared at a doll's head packaged in plastic. The empty sockets stared back at her. "It wasn't me, Julia."

"Nothing else in Quimby has changed. You're the only new attraction."

Attraction was certainly the word for the sparks they struck off each other. The past night, curled against him on the sofa, his arm around her shoulders, the movie had barely registered. Even though he hadn't kissed her again, he'd touched her. A lot. Most of it in a friendly, loving, comforting way. Which was not a common occurrence in her life, but already she was getting used to it. Even to crave it, if her fitful sleep was an indication.

"Ha," said Julia. "You're blushing."

Cathy pressed her knuckles into her warm cheek. "I have to talk to you about Zack."

"You want to know if he's for real."

"Um." Cathy shivered. "Yeah."

"The very question that haunts every one of the Heartbroken." Julia gestured. "Is he real or is he fake? Does he mean what he says, does he genuinely care? Or is it all a game?" She eyed Cathy with a wry little smile. "And then there's the biggie, the one that gives us all a modicum of hope for the future.

"Will he ever fall in love and settle down?"

ZACK PULLED INTO one of the metered Central Street parking spaces and cut the ignition of his black Jag. The car would have to go. For one thing, there wasn't a local garage that could handle the constant maintenance. Secondly, he'd have to cut expenses now that he'd given up his high-paying job. Lastly, he was beyond the flashy-car stage of his bachelorhood.

He shut the door. Paused to pat the hood. It had been fun while it lasted, but he could get used to a minivan if he had to. Particularly one that was filled with a happy family.

The idea was both a big leap and a small step. He'd done fine all these years as a confirmed bachelor, even as he'd known that eventually there would be a woman like Cathy for him—someone whose heart was so open and tender it could encompass all that marriage and family would demand. Julia, for all her estimable worth, wasn't it. Despite appearances, Laurel hadn't even come close, leading him to give up on the prospect altogether. Only after a year away had coming home to Quimby begun to seem like a good idea again.

And bless his luck, he'd found Cathy. Pretty, quirky, sensitive, spunky Cathy. She made his day brighter, his nights...restless. After all his experience, he recognized the signs. He was falling for her, head over heels.

Quite a feat with the specter of Laurel holding him back.

A mass of scudding clouds hid the sun, casting shadows across the street. Zack deposited a quarter in the meter and turned the crank. He nodded at weasel-faced Willie Simms, the town's persnickety pharmacist who insisted on supervising Reggie Lee as the handyman washed the drugstore's plate glass windows. Three women with strollers turned the corner like the vanguard of an approaching army. Recognizing trouble in the form of Liz, the erstwhile bridesmaid, Zack turned and strode along the sidewalk, hoping to get away before they spotted him. He briefly paused to glance up at the unfamiliar sign above the awning—Couturier—before reaching for the door handle, resolute in his decision. This was necessary. It was time.

Showdown.

He wanted to wipe his slate clean, to be the honest, upright, honorable man Cathy Timmerman deserved.

And that meant...facing his nemesis.

Laurel's face went chalky when he entered the shop. After an instant of blazing recognition, she drew herself up and spoke through thin, tight lips. "Well, well, what do you know? If it isn't my dearly departed bridegroom."

Zack shoved his hands into his pockets. This was going to be worse than he'd thought. "Hello, Laurel."

"Hello, Laurel," she mocked. "Don't speak to me, Zachary Brody. I have nothing—*nothing*—to say to you." She spun away, her slender back rigid with tension.

Zack slowly exhaled as he scanned the tony interior of the dress shop. "Nice place. You haven't done badly for yourself, Laurel." Not with a daddy like hers.

Leonard Barnard, Esquire, was the kind of man who liked to be called esquire. He'd welcomed Zack into his family with a hearty, back-slapping show of approval. That was certain to have changed.

"I told you not to speak to me!" Laurel's voice was shrill. She refused to look at him, even when he walked around to face her.

"You know we have to speak."

Her chin trembled as she averted her face. Her hair was slicked back from her face, making her profile look as sharp and stark white as the broken edge on a piece of porcelain. "Don't come near me."

"It's all going to come out," Zack said. "Sooner or later."

Laurel's stricken gaze shot toward a young woman who was lingering over a dress rack, watching them with huge, rounded eyes. For one instant, Zack thought Laurel would crumble.

But no. She gathered herself up again, exuding an air of injured outrage. "Hmmph. What gall. You should be down on your knees, begging my forgiveness."

He recoiled. "*Your* forgiveness? Who do you think you're kidding?"

She slapped her palms over her ears. A spoiled brat, extraordinaire. "I'm not listening!"

Zack made a futile gesture as he stepped away in disgust. "Oh, grow up." Laurel was as beautiful and as selfish as ever. Seeing her like this appalled him. He'd come too close to marrying her, had almost saddled himself with a lifetime of anguish for the sake of duty. Misplaced duty, at that. His mother had been wrong about one thing—a gentleman did not defer to a lady in *all* circumstances.

Laurel's hands shook as she lowered them. She glowered at her employee. "Karen? Take your break."

The other woman's gaze skipped toward Zack. "But, he—you—"

"Leave us alone," Laurel snapped.

The shop assistant brushed past the rack with a metallic clamor and scurried to the door like a frightened rabbit. Zack watched through the window as she hustled along the sidewalk double time, making a beeline for the women on stroller patrol. The power-walking bridesmaid posse closed around her in an avid knot. Oh, hell.

Zack looked away in time to see Laurel advancing on him, her expression fierce. "How dare you come in here," she said, seething, "and *threaten* me."

"I didn't make a threat. Unless..." He met her eyes, "Unless you consider the truth a threat."

Her hand shot out. *Crack.* He took the slap without flinching. The blow had stung his cheek, but not deflected his purpose. "Don't ever try that again," he said, quietly lethal.

"Don't you ever discuss our private business in public," she retorted. Her voice shook, threaded with a hint of fear. "This is a personal matter." Her chin tipped up haughtily, a defensive gesture he remembered. Even Laurel had her insecurities—winding up on the wrong side of public opinion was one of them. "Please try to remember that," she added, clearly grudging the request.

"Sure," he said carelessly. Although she knew darn well their marriage would have been a sham, it seemed she'd managed to keep that part of it quiet. "But then tell me, won't you, why the whole town is bent on blaming me?"

Her brows arched. "Because you jilted me, of course!"

"Is that how you put it?" Revisionist history, he thought. "Considering the circumstances, I'd have presumed you'd be more discreet."

Her face went blank, all but for the spots of burning color in her pale cheeks. "What are you insinuating? Everyone knows that it was your fault. You jilted me on our wedding day!"

The phrase *on our wedding day* slammed into Zack's brain like the slug from a .44, leaving a path of stunning destruction and devastation. He gaped at Laurel in disbelief. "On our wedding day? What the hell are you talking about?"

"I was jilted! On our wedding day! Everyone knows about it! How can you even ask?" Laurel's wail of humiliation bounced off the hard, reflective surfaces of her coldly elegant dress shop. "You stranded me in a church filled with seventy-five guests—it was hardly a private affair!"

Zack was floored. "I did not—"

"What else would you call it?" She seemed beyond hearing his dumfounded protest. Tears streaked her face. For the first time in a year, he felt sorry for her, regardless of her ridiculous claims and counter-claims. "I wa-waited for an hour," she continued piteously. "At the church. In my dress. You didn't show up." *Sniffle.* "My fa-father had to ma-make an announcement to the guests. Seventy-five guests!"

"But, I swear—"

"No. I won't listen to anything but an apology." She grabbed a tissue from behind the sales counter, turned her back and honked.

"Laurel..." Zack shook his head. "Believe it or not, I am sorry—"

"You're just saying that to salvage your sterling reputation," she sneered.

"No. I am sorry. I should have—" He stopped. He didn't want to hurt her, but he had to be honest. Even if it was brutal. "I should have cancelled the wedding much sooner."

Laurel's back stiffened. "Oh. You—you despicable—" She whirled on him, her blotchy face gone furious. "Get...out. Get out." Her demands escalated in pace and volume. "Get out! Get out, get out, get out!"

"WITH ZACK, it's all a matter of personality," Julia said.

Cathy made a face. "You mean it's not his hunka-hunka-burning-love body?"

"Yes, that's part of it. But even the most handsome man in the world can't get by on looks alone. Not forever. And certainly not without leaving behind a mob of angry, vengeful women."

"The Heartbroken aren't like that about Zack."

"Well, no. Except for Laurel."

"Yes, there is Laurel. She was just here, issuing edicts."

"Sorry about that. I tried to calm her down yesterday. But she's feeling threatened by you."

"By *me*?" Cathy said.

Julia's smile was gentle. "You and Zack seem right together, somehow. Laurel recognizes that, even though she won't admit it."

A pleasant calm washed through Cathy. *We are right*, she thought, then immediately hooked on an *I think, I hope, I pray...* If only she could be sure.

"Why would Laurel care? She despises Zack."

"It's the unwritten girlfriend law," Julia said. "You don't date your friend's men, even after they're discards."

"But I—it wasn't my idea to—to—"

Julia hooted. "Gad, Cath. You're so transparent. It's written as plain as day across your face—you're falling in love with Zack."

For an instant, Cathy went stock still. Then she panicked and buried her face in her hands. "You're right. And I don't even know if he's for real. I'm so confused. What if I end up heartbroken? Or worse, despising him the way that Laurel does?"

"That's not going to happen." Julia reached over to pat Cathy's hunched shoulders. "You're not Laurel, for one thing. And you've got Zack all wrong, for another. The main reason he remains universally adored by his exes is because he's so dang nice and sincere." She reflected. "Well, that is, for as long as it lasts, he's sincere. Unfortunately, it doesn't last."

A soft moan. "Why is that?"

"You know, I once asked him that very thing..."

Suddenly Cathy sat up and straightened her glasses.

She knocked her knuckles against her forehead, trying to be cynical. "Stupid question. He's a man—that's reason enough. It's the old seed-spreading excuse." She rolled her eyes with disgust.

Julia was not fazed. "With an ordinary man, you'd be right. They do tend to be focused on only one thing. But with Zack..." Her voice trailed off thoughtfully.

Cathy frowned. "What?"

Julia gave her head a little shake. "Let's just say his reasoning is different from your average gun-shy bachelor."

"Meaning?"

"Meaning the guy actually reveres marriage."

Cathy reared back in surprise. "I don't understand."

Julia shrugged. "Zack's parents have this great marriage. The very model of marriages—a perfect, two-part harmony. They hold hands in public, they kiss and cuddle all the time, they live and act as a synchronized team. I'm not sure that they ever argue, or even disagree, except in a joshing way." Julia sighed. "Spending time with them is enough to make the most cynical, hardheaded feminist crave wedded bliss."

"Oh?"

"So you can imagine what Zack expects from marriage."

Gulp. "Perfection?"

"Pretty much." Julia's shoulders lifted, then dropped as a long sigh gusted through her. "And how's he ever going to find it?"

Cathy rubbed her forehead. "So you're saying that he's a permanent bachelor because..." She hesitated before continuing. "Because...his standards are too high? Uh, like, wow."

"It's a theory."

"Doesn't do much for a gal's confidence."

Julia's chuckle was suitably dry. "So true."

"You aren't lacking in it," Cathy speculated.

Julia lifted one shoulder negligently. Her hazel eyes clouded. "It's not confidence I lack. It's...romance altogether."

"Is that because of Zack? Has he ruined you for other men, the way Gwen always says?"

Briefly Julia clasped Cathy's hands, giving them a reassuring squeeze. "No, Cath. I'm not pining for Zack. If you want to know the truth, it was me who broke up with Zack, not the other way around. I usually don't say so. It's easier calling it a mutual breakup, because—" she spread her palms, made a deprecating face "—nobody believes even that much."

Cathy was struck by a possibility, but felt almost afraid to voice it. "Then...maybe...it's Zack...who's pining for *you?*"

Julia was quick to disagree. "Not on your life. It's true we got on very well. So well that for a time we both thought we'd be capable of emulating Zack's parents. But we never did fall head over heels in love." She slid a sly look toward Cathy. "Not like you two."

Not like you two.

Cathy smiled to herself. Strange, but true. After all the years of dreamy rememberances, it was a shock to find that her hopes had a solid foundation. She and Zack had *it.*

No definition necessary.

The doorbell chimed, announcing a customer. "Cathy?" a voice called out, sounding urgent.

Kay Estress. Cathy checked the timepiece hung on a cord around her neck as she hurried from the storeroom.

Three hours early? "Here I am," she called. "What's up?"

"I was taking my morning constitutional," Kay said briskly. "Thought you should know. Your boyfriend's being accosted right out front of the store."

Cathy put on the brakes. "My boyfriend?"

"The grapevine strikes again," Julia said as she passed. She yanked open the door, craning her neck. "Good grief. Poor Heartbreak."

Quickly Cathy stepped outside. Three women with baby strollers had pinned Zack against her storefront. They were all talking at once, clearly dressing him down even though Cathy comprehended only snatches of the strident lecture. Something about wedding etiquette, bridal gowns and broken hearts. One of them shook a rattle under his nose. Laurel stood outside her shop door with her assistant, Karen Thompson, the latter wide-eyed, the former slit-eyed and smug.

Cathy didn't think. She waded in.

"There you are, Zack." She slipped between a fussy ruffly, hooded baby carriage and a lightweight stroller to grab his arm. "I've been waiting for you," she sang gaily, her voice double its normal volume to override the meddling mothers. "Oops. 'Scuse me, ladies. Coming through. Cute baby."

Once Zack had been towed to safety, she turned and waved to the flummoxed women. "Sorry to steal Zack away from you, but he's needed desperately. Glue gun emergency! I'm sure you understand—seeing as it's a Founder's Day project."

"That was impressive," Zack said below his breath as they entered Scarborough Faire. "Where'd you learn that maneuver?"

"From my father, Admiral Wallace Winston Bell, U.S.N., retired."

Zack's arm snaked around her waist. "Hmm. I'd better keep that in mind next time I'm firing across your bow."

Suddenly Julia was there, hugging Zack. "Hey, Heartbreak. How did you get yourself in such a fix?"

He gave her a lusty squeeze, but Cathy could see that his eyes were dark and his expression grim. "Apparently by jilting my bride-to-be on our wedding day."

Julia laughed. "Even a legendary lover has to take his medicine sometime."

"Laurel wants to commit bloody murder upon my corpse." Zack smiled thinly. "But at least now I understand why I've been getting such a persistent cold shoulder all over town."

Now he understood? Cathy wondered if he'd misspoken, because he wasn't quite making sense. Zack was too gentlemanly not to realize just how dire his infraction of wedding etiquette had been.

"What did you expect?" Julia said with some bite. She fluttered her fingers. "No harm done? Forgive and forget?"

Zack did not explain. "It seems I've been operating under a misconception." He stared at Cathy, his eyes softening. "You're the only one who gave me the benefit of the doubt."

She shoved her glasses up her nose. "Well," she murmured, not quite sure what he was talking about, but definite in her feelings for him, "there was the hateful man Laurel talked of, and then there was you, in the flesh." *And you, in my memory.* "I knew—" She glanced at Julia and Kay and the women who were glaring through the store window at them and stopped, suddenly self-conscious.

Zack planted a kiss on the top of her head and said "Thanks," very quietly, into her hair.

He was so dear. And she was both baffled and miserably guilty. Thanks to her lack of self-esteem, she had allowed herself to become the instrument of Laurel's revenge.

8

WHILE KAY WAITED on customers at the front of the store, Cathy was lost in a sea of purple and white crepe paper at the back. The worktable was mounded with ruffled paper flowers in the local high school's team colors.

Gwen had volunteered Cathy to help out with the decorations for the upcoming Founder's Day celebration. All of Quimby was focused on planning a day of festivities in honor of the early summer day in 1879 when Hiram Quimby had packed up and moved north to get away from his wife, Lovette, forever after referred to in Hiram's diaries as the Battleaxe. There would be a costume parade, a Lovette Quimby "ugly" pageant, a town-wide barbecue and a bachelor auction presided over by an emcee and the winning Battleaxe, followed by fireworks.

All that Cathy remembered from her previous experience with Founder's Day was heat, crowds, rare glimpses of Zack racing by with his friends, and the overwhelming need to throw up the three pieces of coconut cake she'd consumed behind her grandmother's back.

She reflected over the past week while folding another paper flower. Her standing—with both Heartbreak and the Heartbroken—was somewhat of a mystery.

The Wednesday night calligraphy class had been cancelled for lack of participation. Cathy's puppeteers seemed to be making themselves scarce, at least as a group. While she was grateful that she didn't have to explain herself to them regarding Zack, she was also frustrated. His return had raised questions that must be answered.

Her mind kept returning to the jilting. Something fishy was going on there. Something rotten. Ever since the day of her conversation with Julia, she could smell it.

Much as she wanted it to be Laurel who stunk, she couldn't place blame just yet.

Cathy had to admit that her and Zack's conduct had not been exemplary. She'd been less than honest with him and didn't know how to own up to that fact without losing his respect. He was a jilter, whether or not his reasons for skipping out on Laurel on their wedding day were justified.

Despite all this, they'd continued to see each other. Several evenings, they'd sat in his backyard, watching the river, talking and laughing softly, but far more often lapsing into a comfortable silence.

Holding hands and a few lingering kisses was the extent of their physical contact. Though Cathy waited for one of Zack's patented moves—unsure of how to respond—thus far he'd remained a perfect gentleman. There was an unspoken awareness between them. It was like a river current, running deep and silent. She had no doubt that is was strong enough to sweep her away.

To bliss.

And she wasn't sure that she could hold out until all the knots of their relationship were unraveled.

Cathy sighed and went back to the paper flowers. Ten minutes later, Julia and Zack arrived at Scarborough

Faire, and her unmanageable heart leapt at the sight of him.

"Still at it?" he said.

She nodded.

Julia pulled out a chair. "We can help."

Zack said, "Why not?" and scooted Julia's chair beneath her. Cathy demonstrated the procedure and soon they were all folding and fluffing.

"How did it go?" she asked. Julia had shown Zack an office just around the corner.

Julia nodded. "It's a good space."

Zack did not. "It's a blah space."

"It was perfectly fine," she said to Cathy.

"For *Dilbert*," he agreed with a teasing lilt.

"Zack's got something against practicality."

"If I'm going to live and work in Quimby for the rest of my life, I need an inspirational space."

Julia asked Zack the question Cathy had been wondering about. "Why *did* you come back to town?"

He shrugged. "Hey, what can I say? It's my hometown. I missed it."

"What about Adam?" Julia's voice had lowered, but when Cathy's gaze went to her, her sleek head was bent over a half finished purple flower.

"Adam never liked it here."

Julia's head sprang up. "That's not true!"

Zack regarded her thoughtfully. "Maybe you're right. He was happy enough. But he was always restless. You know Adam—he needs constant adventure and stimulation."

Cathy had become familiar with Zack's brother through his stories of their childhood. She knew that until the car accident in Idaho, where he'd gone to do some white-water kayaking, Adam Brody had worked at a variety of blue-collar construction-type jobs to pay for his jaunts to extreme points on the globe.

"What about now?" Julia asked, her voice tight and strained even though she was clearly trying to be her usual unruffled self.

Cathy blinked. *Julia and Adam?* Did Zack know?

When he said, with a gentleness that Cathy found quite touching, "I doubt Adam will ever return, Jule," she was certain that he knew. And that there was more to this story, too. "Not after...everything." He looped a comforting arm around Julia's shoulders.

He referred to the accident, Cathy assumed. And maybe...?

Julia only nodded. But a few minutes later she made an excuse to leave.

Cathy and Zack continued to work. "You see why I feel as though I've landed smack dab in the middle of a soap opera," she said after a while. "And it's rather difficult to catch up." When Zack didn't offer, she put her chin in her hand, looked across the table at him and prompted, "Julia and Adam?"

"Not exactly." Zack's mouth gave a wry twist. "Believe it or not, the story's even more complicated."

"Let me guess. You and Julia were a couple. But somewhere along the way, Julia fell for your brother, Adam. You and she parted company—cementing your reputation as the man who broke a million hearts. Obviously Julia didn't find her happy-ever-after ending with Adam, so that means..." She trolled through the possibilities. "Aha. A fourth party must have entered the picture."

Zack said nothing.

Cathy suspected Laurel, but she didn't get to delve into the ramifications such a quadrangle would have wrought. There was a blond head lurking among the artist's paintbrushes. "Hey, Faith," she said. "Come on over."

Faith approached, looking as jumpy as a frightened doe. She said a soft hello to Cathy and gave Zack a quick, nervous glance.

"Faith Fagan?" he said in a friendly manner, standing to shake hands. "Nice to see you again."

"Hi."

Cathy was sympathetic when Faith looked down at her open hand and blushed. The shy secretary was probably too thrilled by the contact to think straight.

"Why don't you join us, Faith? I've been trying to figure out the ins and outs of the Quimby social scene. Maybe you can fill me in where Zack can't." *Or won't.*

Suddenly Allie darted onto the scene. "Hey, guys!"

"Allie," Zack said. "Where have you been keeping yourself?"

"I've got two kids, a sloppy house and an even sloppier husband." Allie twined an arm through Faith's in a buddy-buddy manner. "You know how it goes."

"Zack's been filling me in on past, uh, relationships," Cathy said. "It seems there are so many complications I'll never completely straighten them out." Neither woman responded, so she plunged boldly onward. Why not get it out in the open? "What I'm really curious about is the wedding fiasco. Laurel's keeping a low profile all of a sudden, so I have my suspicions...."

Zack looked alarmed for an instant, but then his expression became measuring. He inclined his head toward the two women. "You were both there."

"No, I wasn't," Allie said quickly, then frowned. "Where?"

"At Laurel's house the day before the wedding, when

I was trying to get in touch with her. All the bridesmaids were there."

"Oh, yeah, sure, that's right." Gripping both Faith's arm and the strap of her lumpy shoulder bag, Allie nodded eagerly. "No matter how many times you asked, we couldn't let you see Laurel—she was trying on the wedding gown."

"And that was when I left the letter."

Cathy was startled by this pronouncement. *A letter? Zack had left a letter?* Why hadn't he mentioned this before now?

Faith was staring at her shoes.

Allie seemed to be floundering. "A letter?" she croaked.

Zack nodded calmly, as if he hadn't just dropped a bombshell. "I would have preferred talking to her in person, but I had less than an hour to catch a plane."

"Well, cripes, Zack," Allie said, "none of us saw a letter. Isn't that right, Faith?" Faith nodded. "But there *was* a lot of confusion. Six bridesmaids, two pitchers of margaritas. You do the math."

Cathy was calculating the possibilities and topsy-turvy ramifications. "It's possible this letter of yours was...misplaced."

"Possible," he said in a skeptical drawl.

"Sure, of course!" Allie looked relieved. She grabbed a package off a nearby rack and said, "We've got to go," and hustled herself and Faith off to the cash register.

Cathy watched them go before turning to look at Zack, utterly perplexed. "What's all this about a letter? Did you really leave a letter, or were you stirring the pot to see what might bubble up? What's going on?"

"Nothing much." Zack grinned tightly as he scooted

out his chair and sat down. "Just a little character assassination."

"Yours," she guessed. The pieces were starting to fall into place. One by one.

Giving away nothing, he was silent and contemplative for a long while. Finally he dropped another finished flower onto the growing pile and turned toward her, watching her face with an intensity that was unsettling. Gradually his troubled expression cleared. "We have much nicer things to think about than my muddy reputation."

She had no intention of letting him deflect her curiosity yet again, but whenever he looked at her that way, she lost hold of her questions and misgivings.

With the back of her wrist, she nudged her glasses up her nose. Zack had given no sign of noticing a difference between Work Cathy—glasses, pinned-up hair, unappealing apron—and Play Cathy with her sunglasses, loose, shiny hair and much more fashionable wardrobe. Yet he must. No one was that oblivious. He had plenty of experience assessing female appearance.

She didn't know why she'd kept up with her new look, except that she'd gotten to enjoy it. Maybe that was reason enough. The makeover had transformed more than her outer appearance. It had revealed a sense of confidence that must have been lurking inside her all along.

She wanted to be attractive. Not only for Zack's approval, but for herself. As a woman. Not the kind of woman she'd been when she'd married Chad Timmerman, but an incomparable, phenomenal woman.

It was wonderfully liberating.

"Let's think about what we're going to do this evening," Zack said in a low, seductive voice.

Cathy brought her soaring expectations down a notch. "Did we have a date?"

"We have a standing date."

"Hmm. A sitting one might be more comfortable."

Anticipation shone from in his eyes. "Perhaps it's time to progress to a *laying* one?"

"A lay date?" A bubble of silly laughter burst from her. "Is that anything like a play date?"

He reached for her hand. "Exactly like it."

She laced her fingers through his. Already she knew his hand as well as her own—the long, tensile fingers, the crisscross of blue veins at his wrist, the simple gold and black onyx ring he wore on the third finger of his right hand—Quimby High School, Class of 89—the smattering of downy brown hairs that grew across the top. His hands were quick to soothe, even quicker to arouse. When she held his hands, she felt relaxed, protected, comforted. At the same time, she imagined them on her body, drawing pleasure across her skin.

"Sounds good," she said, prickling with sensation. Her skin felt tight and flushed, simply from imagining how their evening might progress. All these days of talking, holding hands, cuddling and sharing no more than sweet pecks goodnight had heated her to the boiling point. The waiting and the thinking had been excruciating. If Zack was finally going to take it up a notch, she was bound to go off like a bottle rocket.

He squeezed her hand. "I'll come over to get you at seven."

Come over to get me?

"There's something I want you to see," he added.

I want to do more than look.

"How does that sound?"

She nodded, quite modestly, her eyes cast downward. *Oh, man!*

ZACK WASN'T SURE exactly when it had happened, but he'd come to realize that he knew Cathy Timmerman better than he ought. At first he'd put it down to natural attraction. They'd been together for most of the past week, as comfortable as old friends, as tentative as new ones. And, at times, as provocatively as any couple that stood poised on the brink of becoming lovers.

It had been difficult, but he'd withheld his desire for her. Partly because he didn't want to rush. Somewhere along the way, it had become vitally important that he get this relationship right.

But it was also because he'd been trying to figure her out. Trying to understand why there was such a compelling link between them.

"What do you think?" he said.

Cathy stood in one of the shafts of sunlight that streamed through gaps in the western wall of the old tumbledown barn. She was especially pretty this evening, her hair sleek and dark against her peachy skin and white shirt. Beneath her brief cotton print skirt, he could see that her legs were starting to tan. The light poured over them like syrup. He swallowed thickly.

Small things about her really got to him—the delicate knob of bone at her ankle, the catch in her voice, the deep blue pools of her eyes when she widened them. He hadn't had a good night's sleep in a week.

"I could say you're a kook." She turned in the sunlight, arms outspread. Tiny, glittering flecks of dust danced all around her. "But *visionary* sounds so much more respectable."

"Visionary? I like that."

"You'd have to be to carve an office building out of this mess." She softened her words with a sweet smile.

The small barn was filled with musty straw bales, rusty farm implements, crusty leather harnesses. Still, it had great bones and proportions—a high ceiling, sturdy beams, a rock foundation. The farmhouse was rubble, but also included were ten acres of open pasture that had gone to seed and a thriving apple orchard. The tangled thickets were alive with fluttering birds. Butterflies flickered among the clumps of buttercups.

"Julia thinks I'm cracked. She likes things to be clean, new and efficient." He pushed his sleeves up to his elbows. "Keeps trying to convince me to be practical."

"Don't be practical." Cathy came toward him, eyes shining, hands outstretched. "It's a great building."

He caught her hands, then couldn't bear the separation and enfolded her in his arms as well so that her arms twisted behind her back. "I used to come here when I was a boy," he said into her sable hair. He pressed a kiss to the white line of her part.

"I know," she murmured, lifting her face to his nuzzling caresses. "Riding your bike..."

He plucked at her bottom lip. "How do you..." Her breasts pressed against his chest, round and soft. He lost the rest of his question in the rising flush of passion.

"I meant—" She tried to tug her arms free but he wouldn't let her. The close contact felt too good. "I can imagine. You were one of those boys who like to explore. Ah, please. Don't do that."

He'd lowered his face to her throat, her upper chest. Her buttons were giving way, her collar spreading wide. He kissed a trail between her breasts and stopped there, the warm perfume of her skin curling in his nostrils. "I can stop." *Don't ask me to stop.*

"No." She shuddered against his mouth. "Don't stop."

He had to release one of her hands so he could scoop a breast out of her conveniently stretchy bra. Her breathing quit, then started again with a gasp when he grazed her nipple with his thumb. The nubbin of tender flesh drew tighter, begging for his mouth by its very prominence.

"You're sure you don't want me to stop?" he said, and his voice ground like gravel. Although he could tell what she wanted by her exquisite response to his caresses, he'd sensed a caution in her that in their present situation would be all too easy to overwhelm. "Last chance."

She moaned. Caught his hand and crushed it to her naked breast. "I want this."

His fingers closed gently around the soft silken flesh. He let go of her other hand, gratified when it settled on his waist. "I've wanted this from the first time I saw you," he said.

Desire pulsed between them in rhythmic waves. "Of course." Her laugh was husky, further inciting his senses. "I was wearing a wet T-shirt."

He whispered, "Before that," then took her mouth at last, in a hungry kiss that didn't come close to soothing his burning need. He wanted her naked in bed, hot and writhing beneath him.

His hand curved around her bottom, snuggling her lower body against his. His erection was so sensitive it was uncomfortable, bound beneath his fly. He felt potent with a raw and primitive lust. Such complete excess was new to him. He'd always been able to contain his physical needs. Always stayed in control, even in the wildest throes of lovemaking.

Cathy was different. Both a lady and a woman. So honest and real. With her, he lost it. He was ragged around the edges, driven by a new sensation he didn't quite dare to identify, even though he knew full well what it was.

She dragged her mouth from his. "Then you *did* see me." She blushed, coming across a tad too indignant for a woman who was half out of her bra.

"I saw everything." He pulled away the stretchy cotton to reveal her other breast.

Her eyes squeezed shut, as if she couldn't bear to look at herself though his eyes. But there was no way for her to avoid his heated voice, his burning touch.

"I saw this." His lips grazed her tilted chin, followed the line of her neck to her delicate collarbone. "I saw these." He closed both hands over her breasts, pressing them together, kneading with his fingertips until an arousal nearly as hot as his own was radiating from her in shimmering waves. "*I saw you.*"

She gave a deep sighing sob and leaned against him, her body lax. He caught her around the waist.

"Kiss me again," she said, parting her lips with a soft wet sound that cut the last string of his control. Acquiescence had flushed her complexion and plumped up her lips. She looked entirely kissable, from every silken hair on her head to the polished toes peeping out of her sandals.

Breathing like a steam train, he covered her lips with his mouth and suckled at them sweetly before opening her wider with a thrust of his tongue, letting the hot charge of lust have full sway. They ground against each other, clutching and awkward, fumbling with haste. Desperate to reach completion at last.

"I can't take this," he said, wrenching himself away.

"Either we go home now or we wind up flat on the dirt floor."

She glanced down, seemed to consider, then lifted her gaze to his. "I guess I'm too practical not to prefer a bed."

He pressed his fingertips to her swollen lips. "Then hold that thought," he said, silently thankful that he still had the Jag.

Zero to ninety in a matter of mere seconds sounded just about fast enough.

"I CAN'T BELIEVE..." Cathy licked her lips; they were supersensitive, as if Zack's kisses had roused a thousand nerve endings she'd never used before. "I can't believe we're going to do this."

The powerful engine of his sports car carried them swiftly toward home. The dark countryside slipped by like water.

"We're just a coupla wild kids." He glanced sideways at her. The glitter of his eyes was diamond-hard and deeply exciting to her maidenly sensibilities.

Cathy's stomach fluttered. She'd started to button up, but he'd said no. He wanted to look at her. So now she sat beside him with her breasts jutting above the wrinkled band of the sports bra, her painfully erect nipples teased by the gentle rasp of the cotton cloth of her undone blouse. The naughtiness of it thrilled her at the same time it worried her.

Squirming in the leather seat, she made a valiant attempt to tamp down her doubts. Not only was she going against her instructions, she was revisiting familiar territory. She'd already flirted with being a bad girl. The result had been Chad Timmerman. Zack was not at all like shallow, faithless Chad, at least not inwardly. But he *was* a heartbreaker.

And she, despite her recent empowerment, would always retain a hint of Cathy Beachball's low self-esteem.

"I was married once," she blurted.

Zack's knuckles went white where they clenched the wheel. "You didn't tell me."

She shook her head, trying to figure a way to get the words out. "It was a stupid mistake. I was only twenty, still in college." The car sailed over a bump and the jog of her sensitive breasts made her gasp. There was a terrible ache between her thighs. Matched only by the yearning of her heart.

She fell silent, one hand pressed to her chest to ease the throbbing need. She couldn't quite catch her breath.

"Want to tell me about it?" Zack asked softly.

She'd been trying not to look at him, but again and again her eyes were drawn to the flexing muscle in his denim-clad thigh and the obvious bulge of his arousal. He was hurting as bad as she, and still he could ask about her past in a voice filled with caring. She knew that he'd even stop if she asked him to. He'd made that clear, and she sincerely doubted that it was a practiced maneuver. His harsh desire had been evident.

Still was.

I do trust him, she thought, testing out the meaning of a different kind of warmth. Making love to Zack would not be a game of seduction and deception. It would be one hundred percent real.

"The marriage lasted only a couple of years. By the time the divorce was final, I'd graduated and moved away to my first job in advertising. I haven't seen my ex-husband since."

"But you have memories?"

"Yes."

"Regrets?"

"Yes."

"Doubts?"

"Oh, yes. Many doubts." She leaned her head against the leather seat. "I changed my life afterward. Or maybe I should say I reverted to the previous one."

"Which was?"

She rubbed her hand across her breasts, too absorbed in answering to think how the gesture looked. "I had always been chubby and shy. I'd moved so often with my father, it was hard to make friends, especially as I grew older and more guarded, knowing that any friendship that developed would soon be broken."

"You haven't mentioned your mother." They were entering the residential district, and he slowed the car accordingly.

Cathy sat forward slightly. Despite the sobering turn of their conversation, her blood still burned. Suddenly she understood that their feelings were not a fraud. They were a vital part of who she was. And who they were, as a couple. Despite either of their pasts.

"My mother died when I was very young. The Admiral raised me alone."

"That must have been difficult for both of you."

"Not so very—on the Admiral's part. He was quite happy to send me away to live with his parents whenever he put out to sea."

"What choice did he have?"

"None. I realize that. Unfortunately, knowing he did his best doesn't change the reality. I grew up feeling unwanted and unloved."

Zack reached for her hand and she let him take it. "Cathy. I'm sorry. I think you're an amazing woman."

Her heart grew wings. Her smile grew wide. "It's funny, but I have been feeling pretty amazing lately."

"Good." He kissed the top of her hand. "You should."

They turned onto Curran Street. In mere seconds, Zack had parked the Jaguar in his driveway and killed the engine. For all of their rush to arrive, neither of them now seemed in a hurry to move.

"Don't tell me about this ex-husband of yours if he was so rotten to you that just hearing about it will make me have to go hunt him down like a dog."

She laughed shortly. "No. The marriage was my failure. I had misrepresented myself to Chad. He thought he was marrying a happy-go-lucky, good-time girl. He didn't know how to deal with the real me—a woman who wanted a home in the suburbs and children instead of sexy careers, tropical vacations and zippy sports cars."

Zack cleared his throat. Then ran his hand along the Jaguar's polished dash.

"Oh," she said. "Sorry. I didn't mean to imply—"

He laughed with some exuberance. "Our inclinations are running along the same channels. But does it have to be a house in the suburbs? Is a house by the river and a barn in the country acceptable?"

She was flustered. Surely promises of forever weren't part of his modus operandi! Or was he simply being glib? "Zack. I—oh, gosh. I don't know what to—"

He held up a hand to stop her babbling. "I'm jumping the gun. You don't have to say anything." The leather seat creaked comfortably as he leaned closer to draw her into his arms. "For now, why don't you just kiss me?"

Her lashes lowered; she was too overcome with emotion to look into his eyes. "I can do that."

"Yes." Slowly he brushed his knuckles against her

cheek while he searched her face. She wondered what he was looking for, dearly hoping that for once she wouldn't fall short.

She cocked her head to the side. Started to speak, then changed her mind. Instead she slanted her lips against his, coaxing him into a deeper embrace with a dozen quick little puckered kisses, then a slow, sucking one that was like drinking a sweet thick mead from a bottomless goblet. Perhaps it was her fancy, but for now she believed there was no end in sight for them. There was only this—loving feelings, hot cravings, depthless desire.

Lost in Zack's skilled kisses, the strong cradle of his arms, she was taken by complete surprise when something that sounded quite large and heavy slammed into the roof of the car.

Blam!

And again. *Blam! Blam!*

She let out a squeak of alarm and shot vertically out of Zack's embrace, jarring her head against the low roof of the car's sporty cockpit. Her jaw slammed shut—painfully. "Ooooch," she keened.

The sound came again, directly overhead. *Blam!*

"Cathryn Bell," a voice boomed. "Front and center!"

Her eyes widened. She knew that voice.

"What is it?" said Zack. He reached over to rub her head, but she ducked away from him to frantically button her blouse.

"Not what," she said as another *blam* rattled the roof. She flinched. A wayward button pinged off the dash. "Who."

Zack looked outraged at the abrupt attack, but her answer stayed his exit. "Who, then?"

"My father," she said with utter misery in the instant before the passenger-side door was yanked open.

Before Zack could respond, an arm shot inside and dragged her unceremoniously from the car.

9

UNFORTUNATELY, Zack realized several minutes later, his earlier comment had been on the mark. We were like wild kids, he thought, seated on the Colton's old lumpy sofa, staring into the reddened face of Admiral Wallace Winston Bell, U.S.N., retired. Unfortunately, instead of getting to do the wild thing, they'd been caught in the act by a stern parent and were suffering the consequences.

Cathy's father set his feet flat on the floor and gripped the thick rolled arms of his upholstered chair. He spared no time in getting straight to the point. With his gaze fixed on Zack, he said in a commanding baritone, "Tell me that you have only honorable intentions, young man."

Zack's smile faded, but then it wouldn't work its usual magic on a man like the Admiral anyway. He cleared his throat. When W. W. Bell said *tell me*, he meant it.

"Yes, sir. I have honorable intentions." Maybe the old guy wouldn't notice the missing word.

Bell's nostrils flared. "I said *only* honorable intentions."

Zack was imagining what would happen if he admitted that his definition of honorable included hot, monogamous, premarital sex, when Cathy reappeared, timing her arrival perfectly. She put a tray of coffee and cookies on the mosaic sofa table that had replaced the Colton's chunky wooden one.

"Cease and desist, Admiral," she chided. "We aren't misbehaving teenagers and this is not an interrogation." Though she'd been as flustered as a schoolgirl when her father had pulled her from the car, apparently she'd used her time in the kitchen to gather her wits. There was a certain stubborn gleam in her eye that matched the Admiral's. Zack's admiration for her ratcheted up another notch. His woman had guts.

The Admiral scowled. He was on the short side, at five-six or seven no taller than Cathy, but his deep voice, rigid posture, tree-trunk body and aggressive presence made a substantial impression. "If a father can't ask these things, who can?"

Cathy smiled determinedly and changed the subject. "Coffee, Dad? I know you like it black. How about a cookie?"

He took a cup, but stared balefully at the flat brown discs she offered. "What are those cookies made of— road tar and pressed cardboard?"

"They're low cal carob wafers."

He took one and dropped it with a clunk on his saucer. "Your Grandmother Bell was a woman who knew how to bake. Fruit pie, cinnamon rolls, coconut layer cake."

"That's so. But all that sugar and fat's not very healthy."

The Admiral's battleship-gray eyebrows knitted together like mating caterpillars. "I'm all muscle." He looked Cathy over. "You appear to be shipshape."

"Thank you, sir." With a small smile, she passed Zack a coffee. "Sugar?"

"Definitely." Under the Admiral's disapproving

stare, he added two heaping spoonfuls to his cup. He tried the smile again, to no avail. "Already we have something in common, sir. We both have a sweet tooth."

The Admiral snorted like a bull.

Zack settled in, draping an arm over the back of the cushions, wrinkling the sari cloth that covered the old sofa. "How long are you planning to stay in Quimby, sir?"

The man inclined his razored gray head toward Cathy, looking almost benevolent. "As long as it takes to be certain my little girl is doing all right."

"I've told you I'm fine."

"Three short calls in the past five weeks? I like regular reports, girl. You know that." Bell's eyes went to Zack. "This child used to send me two letters a week when I was at sea. Now I can't get two words out of her."

Cathy looked wary. "You remember those letters?"

"They were entertaining. Filled with doodles and sketches." The Admiral swallowed some of his black coffee, then let out a satisfactory *ahhh.* "Don't know where she gets the talent."

"It was a way of compensating," she muttered.

"Now then," the Admiral said, overriding her. "What's going on here?"

Uh-oh. Zack sat up a little straighter.

Cathy said hurriedly, "You want an update on the five-year plan?"

Bell had been eyeing Zack challengingly, but he gruffly conceded the point. "That'll do for a start."

Half an hour later, Cathy and the Admiral had gone over every detail of her five-year business plan, including the long-term goals that were not nearly ambitious enough to suit her father, who was a firm believer in setting sights high. Dispatching Cathy, the Admiral went

on to quiz Zack about his own career, scowling over his
resignation from a high-paying job, prodding relentlessly at the "ill-advised" decision to become a country
architect. Surprisingly, the older man didn't dismiss
Zack's descriptive and enthusiastic plans for transform-
ing the barn into an office. Bell agreed that the project
would be a fine showcase of Zack's skills. By the time
they'd decided to call it quits, the two men had acquired
a grudging respect for each other.

Most importantly, they'd avoided talk of more personal issues. Cathy looked duly relieved.

Zack managed a quick word with her at the open front
door. "May I steal a kiss?" he whispered, his hand
reaching around her waist to pull her toward him. "I'm
dying here."

She seemed startled. "Meeting the Admiral hasn't put
a damper on your, uh, enthusiasm? My father had a
knack for reducing Chad to a quivering jelly. He heartily
disapproved of Chad, by the way."

Zack gave an Admiral-like snort. "I'm made of sterner
stuff than that."

She slid her arms around him so that she could muffle
her giggle against his chest.

"I don't wilt so easily," Zack added, his intentions
thoroughly wicked.

Her hips brushed experimentally against his, stirring
his desire anew. "Now *that*, sir, is an exaggeration."

"Give me a minute." Her body was incredibly soft
and round and warm. "Or maybe ten seconds."

"We have to stop." Her lips pursed. "I've got an old
salt with radar ears in the other room."

Zack stroked her hair. "Sneak over to my house after
he goes to bed."

"I couldn't. He'd hear."

"So what? You're an adult."

"An adult who has to meet certain standards."

"All right." He gave her a quick kiss. Hardly any tongue at all. "Whatever you say."

A pent-up breath shuddered out of her. She glanced toward the living room. "Maybe I could..."

"Cathy?" called the Admiral.

She gave Zack a little push. "Go on."

He let his fingers trail across her bare forearm, raising goose bumps. She was so exquisitely responsive.

"I'll be up all night."

Her eyes widened. Just before shutting the door, she vehemently shook her head at him. But she didn't look very convincing, what with her enormous eyes and her lips drawn into a lush pout that only served to deepen the ache in his groin. He really would be up all night. So to speak.

AFTER AN unsuccessful attempt at laying ground rules—the Admiral tended to ignore opinions that didn't support his intentions—Cathy gave up and settled her father into the spare bedroom. They said a crisp, unsentimental good-night, then went one step further and shared a brief, hard hug that made her heart give an unwieldy thump. Feeling pretty good considering she'd left Zack to his own devices, she retired to her bedroom. Her nighttime ablutions were minimal—a quick wash of her face, brushing her teeth, rubbing a little lotion into her work-worn hands.

She didn't get very far.

While kicking off her sandals, she was distracted by the window that faced the Brody house—the one that...well, The One.

Gnawing on her lip, she shimmied out of her skirt and

left it in a puddle on the floor. A quick peek next door wouldn't do any harm.

Except to her resistance.

The bedroom window that she knew to be Zack's was dark. Not a little disappointed, she started to pull the sheer curtains into place. A movement next door stilled her hand. When she looked closer, a sudden, intense burst of heat flared inside her.

Zack stood in the window. His shirt was unbuttoned.

"Oh." She leaned her forehead against the glass. Pressed her palm to it as if she were touching his chest.

He saw her and smiled.

She gave a small wave. He looked so good and so alone her heart filled with turgid emotions. "Oh, Zack," she crooned, wondering if he could see her lips move. "Oh, Heartbreak..."

He put his left hand to the window, the gesture a mirror image to her own. The hammering of her heart was so loud she thought that he might be able to hear.

Acting purely on impulse, she unbuttoned her blouse until it hung open off her shoulders. She dragged a hand across her bare stomach, by then being deliberately provocative. Even across the distance and the darkness of a small-town night, she saw—or maybe simply sensed—Zack's keen reaction. Her body pulsed in response.

In a heartbeat, he was out of his shirt entirely, down to only a pair of jeans by the looks of it. His window was smaller—she could see only to hipbone level. Hers was tall and vertical, framing her figure as far as her knees.

Zack's magnificently muscled torso filled the window. His skin looked pale as moonlight, cast in blue shadows that followed the rippled contours. Her own personal bas-relief map.

When her eyes finally reached his face, he sent her a

wickedly sexy grin and a nod. The message was clear. He'd just upped the ante.

I can play this game, she thought. There were two walls, several doors and a massive rhododendron bush between them. Her father was safely tucked away on the other side of the house, so it wasn't very likely he'd blunder onto her and Zack's naughty little lark.

Plus, there was her status as an incomparable woman to uphold.

Cathy shrugged out of her white cotton blouse. Quick as a flash, she peeled her bra off overhead and tossed it aside with a bold and unfamiliar sense of defiance. Begone her years of low self-esteem and poor body image. She was a woman in charge of her own sensuality!

And Zack—Zack was...well, he appeared to be impressed.

He had one arm propped against the window frame. His head hung forward in astonishment.

She posed for him.

Exhibitionism had never been her fantasy. Yet she couldn't deny that she enjoyed knowing her body was making Zack wild with desire. And that each provocative pose and gesture incited him further.

She skimmed a palm up one thigh, over her torso, stopped to linger at the hollow between her breasts. Across the distance, Zack's dark eyes blazed like coals. Prickling, tingling shivers chased each other across the daringly exposed surfaces of her skin.

She flicked her hair behind her shoulders, pleased by the cool, silken brush of it against her back. Even the smallest sensations were magnified all out of proportion. But the touch she truly craved was out of reach.

Zack. His face was hard. The muscles in his abdomen looked as taut and honed as an Olympic athlete's. He breathed heavily; the rise and fall of his chest was clearly visible.

Playfully, Cathy stroked her breasts, slowly and provocatively at first, then with more pressure. She needed Zack's hands on her, so it wasn't enough. Thinking it would cool down her body temperature, she leaned closer to the window. But the slight shock when her nipples touched the cold glass only made things worse.

She glanced sidelong at the empty street, then checked again on Zack. He hadn't changed position. And he didn't for a full ninety seconds, even though the next move was his.

The wait was excruciating. She pressed her thighs together, aware that she was becoming slick with desire.

Somewhere at the back of her mind was the fear that they'd gone too far, but, oh, how she ached to continue.

She ached all over.

Zack dropped his hands to his waistband, popping the snap, giving her a glimpse of white cotton briefs. Cathy's heart skipped a beat. He didn't stop. He didn't hesitate. Although her view was not complete, she was certain that he had unzipped and slid the jeans and briefs down his lean hips. He bent at the waist to step out of them, then straightened with a wad of denim in one hand. One flick and they were gone. Tossed aside.

He was—*gulp*—naked as a jaybird. She couldn't see everything. But she could see just enough to know he was…aroused.

He didn't touch himself. He simply stood there, devastatingly male, blatantly virile, arms hanging at his sides until he extended one and slowly beckoned her with the languid furling and unfurling of a crooked finger. He didn't speak, but she knew what he was saying.

Come to me.

If only he knew how far she'd already come to be with him.

Cathy smoothed a palm over the curve of her belly, wondering if she dared. She was not herself. Or perhaps she was, a version of herself that she'd never met before. *Cathy in Love.* So deep in love she could forget all her nagging fears.

She hooked her thumbs in the elastic waistband of her bikini panties, started to go south, then suddenly reversed direction. She pulled the elastic taut to her waist, snapping it in place like suspenders.

Enough with the teasing. It was time to go to him.

She gestured to Zack, pointing toward his back porch. He disappeared from the window at once.

No backing out now.

She put on an oversized nightshirt—she wasn't *that* daring—and cracked the bedroom door. All clear. Tiptoeing, she made her way along the hall and down the staircase, each creak striking fear into her heart. Briefly she stopped to trace Zack's initials carved in the newel post—by now a habit that she considered a good luck charm. No sounds of life had come from her father's room, but it wasn't until she'd stepped outside and soundlessly closed the wheezy screen door that she dared to draw breath.

The rhododendron bush rustled. *"Psst, Cathy."*

"Zack!" She lowered her voice to a harsh whisper. "What are you doing out here?"

"Coming to get you." A branch snapped.

"For goodness sake, stay where you are." She ran through the cool grass, skirting the bush entirely. Zack stood bare chested amidst it, his thick hair wildly tousled and his grin at its cockiest. She eyed his bare feet and legs. The blossom-laden branch that covered his lower body. "Are you...?"

"Sure am."

The neighboring yards were dark and quiet. The glow of the streetlamps didn't reach between the houses, so they were relatively safe. "What if someone saw?"

"Then they'd know for sure I've gone round the bend for Cathy Timmerman."

She shook her head. "I don't do things like this."

Zack reached out to snag her hand. The branch bobbed dangerously. "You were doing a pretty good job of it up in that window." He pulled her closer and desire broke through her in delicious swoony waves. Twigs snapped; falling petals brushed softly against her legs. She could *say* she wasn't the type, but recent evidence was testifying otherwise.

"I don't want to mislead you," she whispered into his chest, the feel and scent of warm male flesh overwhelming her. She clutched his hard biceps. "That's what happened with my ex-husband."

"I know who you are."

She nearly sobbed. "You don't—"

"I know everything about you." His tone brooked no argument. With gentle fingers, he tipped up her chin. "Believe me."

The heat of his stare was searing. She wanted to close her eyelids, to look away, but she didn't. She hung on. She met his eyes unblinkingly, feeling as though he was looking straight into her soul, seeing all of her at once. And that he was loving her. That he found her flaws and human foibles as beautiful as her long hair or slim waist or flaunted breasts.

Zack lowered his mouth to hers. She rose on the balls of her feet to meet him, drawn inexorably. They lost themselves in the kiss for many minutes, until there was no existence but their own.

"We'd better—go—inside," Zack eventually said between wet, plucking kisses.

"Mmm." She was sunk deep into bliss and didn't want to surface.

"You first." He waggled the crushed branch so it flipped up the hem of her nightshirt.

That got her attention. She looked down. "Unh. I see what you mean." Her glasses slid along her nose. She pushed them back up. Although the branch was rather mangled, she couldn't quite see *all* that he meant.

"I'll take those." He removed her glasses.

"Hey."

He turned her by the shoulders. "Go on."

They walked to the back door, Zack keeping pace right behind her. Cathy couldn't stop giggling—until they were inside and he quickly slammed the door and pressed her up against it. Her glasses clattered to the floor. "I've never gone to such extreme lengths for a woman," he said, and brought his mouth down on hers with devastating skill. She was darned if he didn't kiss all the amusement right out of her.

Maybe not all. She tore her mouth away and said, panting, "Glad I'm the one getting the full length."

His eyes were black in the dim light. Black and fierce. He put his hands on her bottom, squeezed lustfully, said, "Not yet you haven't," and lifted her hips higher. The nightshirt was bunched at her waist and his thigh wedged between hers to open her legs. She had one instant of separate exposure and then he was tight upon her and she felt the entire hot pulsing length of him pressed against her belly. Her skin shuddered and her blood sang in her veins, all heat rushing to coalesce in the spot where they touched so intimately.

No intelligent response was possible. One of her legs dangled over his thigh, the other made contact with the floor by the grace of one searching toe. All she could do when he tugged at her nightshirt was raise her arms and let it go.

He looked at her breasts. She arched her back to thrust them forward, never so naked and assured at the same time.

"You're perfect," he said, looking into her eyes. His gaze held her as surely as his embrace.

The back of her head hit the door with a thunk at the shock when suddenly he swooped in to open his mouth over one breast and pull her nipple into a wet warmth, sucking it hard against his fluted tongue. His teeth raked her flesh. She hunched her shoulders. Tried to dig her nails into the wooden door. *"Zachary."*

He eased up to let her catch her breath, raining tender kisses along her throat. "I knew this was coming. But I wanted it to be pretty and romantic and special..." She felt him swallow. "For you."

And she was under orders for this not to happen at all. "I knew it was coming, too." She rested her elbows on his shoulders and skimmed her fingers through his wavy hair. "And right now I don't care about pretty and romantic." Another shudder rippled through her. "Being with you any way at all is special enough." Her voice shook. "I just want to do it." She could worry about the rest of it afterward.

His fingers slid over her curved buttock, lowering her panties with a sweeping caress. They shifted against each other in a glissade of damp friction. "Do you have protection?'' she asked, because in another sixty seconds she wouldn't care.

Zach froze with a fistful of her underwear pulled half-way down her thigh. ''Damn. I forgot. Upstairs. In my jeans.''

''Oh, no.'' Cathy slithered limply against him. She couldn't make it all the way upstairs.

''Wait. There's one in the other room. In the pocket of a jacket.''

''Salt them away everywhere, do you?''

''That's good, isn't it?'' He put his hand between her legs.

She inhaled sharply. ''Very good.''

His fingers brushed over her damp curls. His cocked hips held her thighs apart, even when she squirmed with the urge to close them tight. She rocked against the invading pleasure as he stroked deeper, easing two fingers inside her where she felt soft and liquid and warm. His thumb nudged at her clitoris, sending a stinging jolt of electricity upward. She stiffened. Drew air through her clenched teeth.

He took his hand away and pressed her firmly against the door. She blinked, stunned by the abrupt change, until just as suddenly he dropped to his knees and opened her again with one palm on the back of her thigh. Stunned by the erotic position—by its sheer intimacy— she managed only to slide a loving hand through his hair, then gripped it at the roots when he boldly nuzzled into her femininity. His tongue was as assured as his fingers. It lapped inside her, over and over again, then withdrew to swirl and suckle and flick at her pleasure points until the hot surging waters had closed over her head and she was lost in the darkest depths of desire.

Her entire body strained upward, reaching for the

calm surface. Yet again and again she was dragged down, all sensation concentrated on one point. The center of the vortex.

He didn't stop.

"Mmm," she crooned. "I'm coming." She closed her eyes and exhaled slowly, the last of her air hissing through her teeth as she searched blindly with outspread fingers for something to hold on to. Zack reached up and caught her hand. She gripped so tight her nails bit half-moons below his knuckles.

The climax washed over her in hard, crashing waves. She abandoned herself to it, barely aware that Zack was on his feet, holding her up, his hand still stroking between her legs to ease the way.

She put her face against his chest and squeezed her closed eyes shut even tighter. Occasionally a shivering spasm coursed through her. "Why did you do that?"

"I wanted to worship you."

She couldn't imagine that. "No, really."

He draped one of her limp arms around his shoulders and began walking her through the dark house. "I wanted to set you free, watch you soar."

Oh, she had. Unbelievably. "But, we—"

"Shh." He deposited her on an overstuffed sofa. "We have plenty of time."

"No. We don't." She struggled with her thoughts, still half at sea. "There are so many things I—"

"Shh." Zack pressed a kiss onto her lips as if he was sealing an envelope. "Don't talk. Don't worry. Don't move." He tweaked her nipple between his thumb and forefinger and it hardened again instantly. He patted her breast. "I'll be right back."

"Mmmph." She opened one bleary eye, but without glasses her view of his disappearing backside was sadly out of focus. She turned and pushed at an oversized pillow. She didn't want to be on a couch. She wanted to make love with Zack in a bed. Like real lovers.

But the curved staircase was daunting. And she was nude, unless you counted the coil of underwear clinging to her right ankle.

She sat up, kicked away the panties, found a fringed throw that had been draped across the back of the floral chintz sofa.

The reality of the situation was starting to hit her. And it was faintly embarrassing. Zack had been in charge. She had only surrendered to the explosion of sensation.

Not good enough.

Cloaked in chenille, she climbed the carpeted stairs. Zack had stalled at the top, muttering to himself as he tried unsuccessfully to tear open the foil packet. Oddly, that gave her confidence. Despite his Prince Charming persona and the perfectly honed body, Zack was not perfect. Even he could fumble and swear.

He started to descend. She met him, stopping him with a hand to the chest. "Where do you think you're going?"

"Hunh?"

"I want you in a real bed."

His eyes opened wide. He stared at her face, then down at the chenille throw. "Uh, sure."

"Then show me the way," she said, thinking that he already had.

10

ZACK SQUEEZED the end of his nose, keenly aware of his nudity. Which wasn't something that would normally bother him, but stripping for Cathy had given him a new perspective. And now she was sitting on the edge of his bed, hugging the knitted throw around herself, and staring at him. Quite intently.

"May I touch you?" she said.

"Uh, yeah." He smiled sheepishly. Did she think he'd say no?

She saw the smile. "I know it's a stupid question. But you have such good manners, I didn't want to—"

"Good manners extend only so far." He took her face in his hands and kissed her. "Please, may I touch you?"

Her gaze skittered away. "You already did." She reached out from beneath the blanket and ran her fingertips up his leg. Her smallest touch got big results from his body. Every hair prickled. His erection swelled. Uncomfortably. He closed his eyes and tried to focus on something remote and dry like baseball statistics, but it was impossible. Cathy's hand brushed across his abdomen. His muscles jumped. A fingertip dipped into his navel, then stroked downward, following the line of hair that led—

Mercy. Her hand closed around his shaft. He gritted his teeth, asking again for mercy. For reprieve. He couldn't take it.

She released him.

"Zack?"

He opened his eyes and looked down at her, sitting on the edge of the bed with her legs tucked beneath her. The blanket had parted to reveal her breasts, and the rosy nipples that tasted like heaven on earth. Her black lashes lifted to allow her clear blue eyes to bore into his. "Should I—" She bit at her bottom lip, then reached out again and stoked her thumb over the throbbing tip of his erection. "You know. The condom?"

The torn packet was gripped in his fist, forgotten. "Right." He forced his fingers open. "I think it would be better if I did it."

"All right." Her arms wound around him from behind when he sat on the bed. She licked his shoulder, peppered kisses behind his ear. He fumbled with the condom, all thumbs in his haste. He was like a virgin again—so eager and awestruck he'd lost his cool. He puzzled at that, then understood why. Being with Cathy meant so much to him, it was like the first time all over again.

She was the woman he'd been looking for all his life.

"Sweet girl," he groaned, turning toward her.

"Zack?" Her voice was wondering.

"This is it." He kissed her, and as he did he pressed her down onto the bed. Her body curved into his, warm and relaxed.

"Mm-hmm." She sighed with satisfaction. "This is it." Though her eyes danced in the light of the small lamp he'd put on, her expression was faintly quizzical. Bless her heart. She didn't understand how thoroughly he knew her, how deeply his desire was rooted. But she'd soon find out.

She cupped her breasts, offering them to him like

fruits of the earth. He feasted for long, luxurious moments, wanting to give her as much pleasure as he gave himself. She shuddered beneath him, clutching at his shoulders, her hips twisting restlessly. He hooked his hands behind her knees and spread her legs apart, settling himself between them with such a sense of assurance that the moment went to his heart and stayed there, as solid and everlasting as he'd known it would be.

He stroked one finger, then another, into the soft, pink, swollen center of her. A warm dew drenched his fingers. She moaned and writhed against his hand, her head thrown back against the pillow.

He sought her eyes. "Look at me, Cathy, love."

She watched him from beneath sultry, half lowered lashes. Her lips parted, but she didn't speak.

It didn't matter. He knew. *This was it.*

She was his, he was hers. Even though there were plenty of deceptions between them, about this there was not a shred of doubt in his heart. He loved her, would love her forever. That was the key—what he'd been leery of facing up to.

No more.

He guided himself forward, then slowly pushed inside her by excruciatingly minute degrees until they were fused as one. Her body was incredible—smooth, tight, clasping him in velvet warmth. Seeking to distract himself from the fire building in his groin, he laced his fingers through hers, covered her face in kisses. She wrapped her silken legs around his waist, tightening intimately around him so he couldn't deny the urge to thrust deeper.

"I can't hold back," he muttered, breathing in her scent as he pressed his face to her arched throat. In its hollow, he found a pulse that matched the one he'd touched deep inside her.

"Then, please..." She rubbed her belly against his, the motion of her hips inciting him to plunge again and again until he was there, deeply there at the vital heart of her. He came with a shout and she rocked him in her arms as the power of his climax broke over him in hot shuddering waves.

Sated, he rested for a moment upon her, suffused with a primal masculine triumph. Gradually the sound of Cathy's harsh, panting breath worked its way past the drumming of his own heart. He moved experimentally inside her. She caught her lip between her teeth. He stroked a path down her body and her satiny skin quivered beneath his palm.

"You're on the edge," he said, levering the back of her thigh to open her to his touch.

She gasped and covered her eyes with her arm. "Hurts."

"But it's such a good pain." He gave a sudden, sharp thrust and she came with a shocked cry that flew from her lips like a wild bird set free. He hugged her the way she had him, embracing her with his entire body. She whimpered, and he soothed her trauma, softly biting and sucking at her mouth and throat and breasts until she was limp and soft, replete with satisfaction. Then he drew the soft wool blanket over them and held her close beneath it as they drifted into a blissful sleep.

HE AWOKE with a start sometime later to find her standing by the window, tilting a framed photo toward the light. "What are you doing?" he asked softly, and she jumped, clasping the photo to the front of her nightshirt. The fabric pulled taut across her breasts, making him sorry she'd felt the need to dress. At least she hadn't gone home.

"I have to go," she said.

"Not yet."

"My father—" She shrugged. "He might notice I'm missing."

"C'mere." Zack stretched out an arm to her.

Her glance was shy as she quickly scanned his supine position on the double bed. They hadn't made it all the way between the sheets, but they'd sure rumpled up the covers. "I was looking at your trophies," she said. Three dusty shelves full of them, chrome-plated testaments to his athletic prowess, each topped with small silver or gold figures of swimmers and basketball players. They were relics of his high school days—a fixture in the room he'd rarely noticed. "And this photo," she said, brandishing it. "Your parents?"

"Let's see."

She came closer to show it to him, a color portrait framed in silver. "Right," he said, "my parents," and slid his palm along the back of her smooth thigh, remembering how he'd opened her legs, how finding his place between them had been more exalting than winning a mere trophy could ever be.

Cathy's skin rose into goose bumps, so he knew she was affected even as she said wistfully, "Your mother is stunning."

"I guess so." This wasn't the time to talk about his mother.

"But your father..."

Oh, well. Zack's chuckle was rusty. "He's not a prize, huh? At least not physically."

"He's short and kind of...well, funny looking. I'm assuming you didn't inherit your looks from the Brody side of the family.''

"Yeah, well, Mom always said she didn't marry him for his genes, but to tell the truth, I don't think she particularly cared about his looks. You know how it is. Once you know a person, you grow accustomed to their face—it takes on its own character. A bad personality can make the most beautiful face seem ugly.''

"I like that attitude.'' Cathy sat on the bed. She put the photo on the nightstand and smiled down at him, her dark hair falling around her face.

She was completely beautiful to him.

So beautiful he felt as though his heart had split in two. She had half, and only when they were together, really together, was he going to be whole again.

Damn. What was with him, thinking in such schmaltzy terms?

He tried to swallow the lump in his throat but it wouldn't go down.

Cathy ran a finger over one of his eyes. "Wet," she whispered, and leaned over him to kiss each lid. He tilted his head back to reach for her lips. She made a soft sound of yearning and opened her mouth for him. He drank from it, his mind reeling with the beautiful whole of her, her scent, her body, her eyes, her tender heart and fascinating mind. They had so much to talk about, but for now talking was not his first priority.

"I want to know everything about you," she said when they broke off the kiss. She was lying on top of him, breast to chest, belly to belly, layering him with feminine heat.

"Thought you already did." He pulled a face. "The grapevine.''

"No." She propped herself up a bit. "I'm not talking

about the suave heartbreaker and All-American Boy Scout everyone else sees. I want to know the real you."

He pushed her nightshirt up to her waist and feathered caresses over the smooth round muscles of her buttocks. "What if that's all there is?"

"It's not." She wiggled against his thighs, and he felt himself growing hard. "Tell me about how you learned to swim. I want to know about your first kiss, the name of your pet dog, your favorite Halloween costume, the dreams you had sleeping in this very bed."

"I can tell you about the time I stood up in front of the fifth grade and recited the Gettysburg Address with my shirt on inside out," he said, wondering if she'd counter with the secret that he'd already guessed. How much did she trust him?

Her eyes clouded. "Sure."

The clock beside the bed ticked off several seconds as he waited, watching her troubled face. She took everything to heart. He loved that about her, even knowing it caused them complications. Part of him wished she didn't need proof of his good character, that final piece of the puzzle which he still couldn't tell. He wanted her to look into his eyes and know all that was irrelevant except the love that had grown between them.

He put his arms around her and turned her onto her back. Pushed the loose nightshirt up even higher, past her breasts. Her skin was white as milk in the moonlight. "It's all right," he said, soothing her with long, loving strokes. "We have all the time in the world."

She tensed. "Do we?"

He stopped licking at her nipple. "Why not?"

"No reason." She wound her arms around his shoulders, holding on so tight he felt the small quaking shivers that coursed inside her as he eased her legs apart. "No reason at all."

WHEN CATHY let herself in the back door beneath a rosy gray sky, she came upon the Admiral sitting at the kitchen table in a white sleeveless T-shirt, unbelted chinos and bare feet. His jaw bristled with white whiskers. Blue veins gnarled his ankles and feet; his toe nails were thick and faintly yellowed. She was so startled by this vision of the less-than-impeccably-pressed Admiral that she forgot to be intimidated.

"Morning," he said.

She crossed one leg over the other. "Morning."

The Admiral, bless his cast-iron heart, plowed full speed ahead. "Tell me one thing. Does your young man have the balls to make an honest woman of you?"

Good grief.

"I—uh—tha-that's—" She stopped and swallowed and tried again. "I'm already an honest woman, Dad."

There were only two times in her life that she hadn't been. At twenty-one, when she'd turned herself inside out for the sake of appearance and popularity. And again, more recently. For Zack. But not *with* Zack. Every moment with him had been honest and good and real.

She squared her shoulders. Lifted her chin. She was the daughter of an admiral, after all. And this time not even his disapproval could diminish her.

W. W. Bell scowled. He got up from the table with a small grunt and came at her, strutting like a bantam rooster.

Her heart hammered, but she held her ground.

He pulled up, inches away. "You'd best marry him."

"Why?" she said, expecting a lecture on proper conduct, old-fashioned family values, truth, justice and The American Way.

The Admiral huffed. "Because the poor guy's lovesick as a newlywed sailor." He turned and pulled out the coffeepot before it had finished dripping and poured himself a cup.

Cathy boggled.

"Then there are my grandchildren to consider." A familiar steely blue glint lit the Admiral's eyes. "A proper upbringing is crucial." He took a breath to launch into the appropriate lecture, but Cathy didn't give him the chance to begin.

She socked him in his muscled gut.

He took a step backward, startled, but not hurt. He blinked. Then he threw back his head, his nostrils flaring. "Go on, give it another try."

She shook her hair back and jabbed again. There had been little physical affection between them when she was growing up, but the one thing she remembered was how he'd suck in his gut, declare himself the toughest guy in the Navy and dare her to take her best shot. She was no boxer, but he'd usually manage to cajole her into it. There had even been times her punches were fueled by resentment more than playfulness. Maybe, she thought, taking another gentle jab before the contact dissolved into a hard but comforting hug, he'd known that all along.

SEVERAL YEARS BEFORE, Allie and Fred Spangler had built a new house in the area unofficially known as "The Country Club." There was no actual country club, just an unchallenging nine-hole golf course that was open to the public, bordered by the thin green ribbon that was Laretta Creek. The Spangler house, a shingled two-story

ode to the Prairie style as designed by Zack, overlooked
the stand of cypress trees that set off the eighth green.

Despite a dearth of domestic skills, Allie liked to play
Lady of the Manor. Even though Zack's last-minute invitation to dinner had come from Fred and she wasn't
happy about it—he'd overhead them arguing in the
kitchen—she'd taken the time to remove their meal from
various take-out containers, nuke it in the microwave
and place it on real, albeit plastic, plates. They ate on the
deck outside, beneath an umbrella that creaked and
flapped in the wind.

Zack had a dinner companion. Four-year-old Lucy
Spangler sat on his lap in a slightly damp bathing suit
for the entire meal, refusing to budge, so he tickled her
pudgy kneecaps and fed her baby shrimp and slivers of
water chestnuts. When Fred picked her up, she cried
and clutched handfuls of Zack's hair until Allie bribed
her with an orange Push-up and *Pocahontas.*

"Woo-hoo, another conquest," Allie said, watching
Zack blot his lap with a paper napkin.

"She's a cutie."

Fred came back outside. "Lucy's in love. She wants to
know if you'll marry her."

"Poor kid." Allie rolled her eyes. Fred tried to pat her
head as he circled the table and she batted his hand
away. "Zack's good at engagements. It's the follow-
through that needs work."

"You're still mad at me," he said, slightly stunned. Allie had always been his pal, almost like a sister even
though it was true that they'd shared their first kiss.
Kisses, he corrected, fondly remembering their clumsi-
ness. But that had been just before puberty hit with a
bang and he'd discovered the allure of seventh-graders
with long shiny hair and budding breasts.

"I'm not mad." Allie's lip stuck out. "Laurel deserved all that she got."

"No," Zack said. "She did not."

"Ya figured out that whole mess yet?" Fred asked, slumping in his chair and spreading his arms in a lazy stretch.

"I'm not sure it matters anymore," Zack said, watching Allie from the corners of his eyes. "I can shoulder the blame. As long as the people who matter understand that I didn't intend for Laurel to suffer so publicly." He hesitated. "Allie...?"

"I never blamed you," she said hotly, staring fixedly at the edge of the table. "I've been standing up for you all this time. Even when there wasn't a word from you. Not one word!"

Zack sighed. "I'm sorry about that. For a long time, Adam's condition was all that I cared about. I tried not to even think—" He broke off, shook his head. Laurel's twisted manipulations had taught him a hard lesson. His life had been a smooth ride up till then, he knew that. Whether it was good genes, the luck of the draw or the grace of God, he'd been blessed.

"It's water under the bridge," he said, trying to pass off the awkward moment. "I appreciate your continued friendship, Allie."

She moved around in her chair. "Sure."

For a moment, Fred's face was expressionless. Then he put on a sly smile. "Talk's spinning the Quimby gossips 'round like tops. I hear Lucy's got a rival for your hand."

Zack looked to the right at the fluttering leaves of a young maple. He smiled.

Fred scratched his sandy yellow curls. "Still can't figure this one out, man."

Peripherally, Zack saw Allie turn her head aside. She suppressed a smile. A smile of a different sort. An unpleasant sort?

"Cathy Timmerman," Fred wondered, oblivious.

"Well, cripes, have you seen her lately?" Allie said. "Fred, you can be as dumb as a box of rocks."

"Huh?"

Allie threw up her hands, exasperated.

Zack frowned. "What are you saying?"

"You, too?" Allie scoffed. "*Men.* Honestly, Zack, with all your experience with the opposite sex, can't you tell when you're being played like a fish on a line?"

"Cathy's not that type—"

"Oh, yes, she is. She's been getting lessons from Laurel. Didn't you know?"

Zack's gut dropped like an elevator, except there was no bottom. It just kept dropping and dropping and dropping.

"Allie," he said tightly, "tell it to me straight. What do you mean?"

Allie flushed. "Well, there's the, uh, makeover. You must have noticed the change in her appearance?"

Zack waved a hand. Makeup and wardrobe meant nothing to him. The only thing he'd particularly noted was the appearing and disappearing glasses, but he thought Cathy looked like a cuddly, sexy bookworm in glasses. He'd taken to adding to a mental list of 101 ways to steam them up.

"Yuh, I sure have," said Fred. "Hotchacha!"

Allie shrugged. "So, there."

Zack's jaw clenched. "But what about Laurel?"

A tense silence followed.

Allie's face squinched up. It always did when she was trying to wiggle her way out of a fix of her own making.

"All I meant was that Laurel helped Cathy with the makeover." She cleared her throat. "We all did, sort of."

"We?"

"Oh, golly. You know. Me, Julia, Faith, Gwen..."

"They meet at Scarborough Faire every Wednesday and call themselves the Heartbroken," Fred said with a snippety tone that undercut his usual laissez-faire pronouncements. "Ain't that cute?"

Zack swiped a hand over his face. *The Heartbroken.* Sheesh, what must Cathy think of him? And why had she surrendered herself to their clutches?

"Heartbreak's got himself some groupies—"

"Fred," Zack said. "Shaddup."

Fred leaned forward to put his elbows on his knees, his fists clenched between them. "Yeah," he said softly, staring off into the middle distance above his wife's head. "Whatever."

"Sorry, buddy."

Fred's shoulders slumped. "Not your fault."

Allie's face had slowly crumpled to dismay. "It's just a...a...thing. A joke."

"And Laurel's involvement?" Zack said as he rose. "Do you believe she was joking?"

Allie didn't answer. She was looking at Fred's stricken face with a dawning awareness, realizing that perhaps Fred was not as accepting of her Heartbreak fixation as he'd made out to be.

Zack swore silently at himself. Clearly, all was not well between Fred and Allie, and he couldn't help but wonder if his return was somehow to blame. Did she harbor feelings for him? Was she clinging to romantic notions after all these years?

Was it possible that she'd played a part in the mix-up

about the letter that had led to his supposed jilting of Laurel Barnard?

Whatever the case, Zack could see that his smooth ride through life had come at the expense of the bumps, bruises and inner turmoil of those around him. Not for the world would he have purposely caused this friction between his married friends, but there didn't seem to be a way for him to solve it. They'd have to do that for themselves.

Leaving them to it, he said his thank-yous and good-byes, giving Fred's shoulder a firm squeeze as he passed.

Cathy was on his mind as he drove away. He remembered the little scene the women—the *Heartbroken*, he thought with a grimace—had set up in her backyard. The meaning of it hadn't occurred to him before. He'd thought it was just one of those mystifying things women did in the name of romance. Usually he paid closer attention to the details. Women liked that. But on the night in question, he'd already been enamored with Cathy and she with him. And he would have sworn on a stack of Bibles that it had been that way from the first time they looked into each other's eyes.

They hadn't needed any extra impetus to fall in love.

So why was Laurel involved? She swore she despised him.

Was he going to have to reveal all the ugly truths he'd been holding back?

Zack slammed the car into gear and sped toward Quimby. He had a very bad feeling about this.

11

"ON A SUNNY DAY in June of 1879, Hiram Quimby stumbled out of the woods with an ax and a bedroll," Gwendolyn Case recited without needing to glance at the sheaf of papers in her hand. "He stopped to feast his eyes upon the body of water we now know as Mirror Lake—" she swung her arm like a game-show model, indicating the sparkling blue lake "—falling to his knees in praise of its wondrous natural beauty." By virtue of her booming voice, Gwen had been named Master of Ceremonies for the fifth year running.

Cathy kneeled before the plywood platform that was the temporary stage and began gluing purple and white crepe paper carnations to the raw edge.

"'Feast his eyes?'" said Allie, who was tacking up a rather bedraggled fringed Mylar skirt in advance of the encroaching carnations. "'Falling to his knees?' Gimme a break. Who wrote that?"

"I did." Gwen lowered the pages with a *harrumph*. "Five years ago. Nobody else has complained."

Allie's lips pursed. "Okay, fine by me," she muttered, duck-walking another few feet, unrolling the fringe as she went. She gave it a yank and shot it into place with the staple gun.

Cathy picked up a purple paper flower. She'd noticed that Allie was not her usual sassy self, but now wasn't the time to ask. They'd been fixing up the pageant stage since 8:00 a.m. Allie had already announced she had to leave in time for the parade—both of her kids were riding decorated bikes in it.

"Maybe you could say, 'He gazed in wonder' instead," Cathy suggested, uncertain why she cared. She was willing to donate her time for the Founder's Day celebration, but the events themselves weren't her cup of tea. She was a behind-the-scenes sort of person. No makeover could change that. And that was okay with her.

"Kinda blah," Gwen said.

Not really. Cathy smiled to herself, thinking of Zack. She'd found a guy who loved her for herself.

Allie's eyes narrowed. "What's up with you, Cath?" She sounded peevish.

Cathy stuck on another purple flower. "Give me an excuse to play with crepe paper and I'm a happy camper."

Gwen peered down at them. "The school colors are supposed to alternate. Purple, white, purple, white," she said helpfully.

Cathy examined her handiwork. "Oops."

"Like it matters," Allie said.

"Geez, what happened to you? Get up on the wrong side of the bed?"

"Just the usual aggravation." Allie glanced across the beach parking lot, where Fred and Zack were helping to nail together the carnival booths.

Cathy's eyes followed the same path. Even though it was early yet, the sun was blazing. Zack had stripped off his shirt and tied it by the arms around his waist so it hung loosely around his denim-clad legs. He wore a pair of stylish black sunglasses and a Quimby Kingpins baseball cap—backward. He looked young and virile and competent in a thoroughly masculine way. Rich emotion stirred inside her at the sight of him, not a little of it basic animal desire.

"Geez Louise, will you look at Heartbreak?" Gwen said. "That man could melt an iceberg."

It was true, he looked totally hot. Cathy stuck three more purple carnations in place without noticing. Neither did Gwen, who plunked down on the stage to man-watch, or Allie, who was looking in the same direction with her freckled face squeezed into a knot.

Eventually Gwen nudged Cathy. "How's that seduction business coming along? It's been *days* since we've had a report."

"Umm." She carefully selected a white flower. "There's really nothing to report."

Allie's gaze darted nervously—or so it seemed to Cathy. There were odd vibrations in the air, but she couldn't figure out why. Even Zack had seemed off-center since he'd come back from dinner with the Spanglers, although he'd taken care to be as winning as ever. Which had been the difference, Cathy thought. Being charmed by Zack was usually as natural and easy as basking in sunshine.

"Nothing?" Gwen was incredulous.

"That's what she said," Allie snapped. "Leave it alone."

"Tell that to Laurel," Gwen said. "Here she comes."

Cathy looked up. Laurel was as lovely and pristine as ever in a floaty chiffon dress with strappy sandals. She led the triumvirate of women Zack referred to as the bridesmaid posse, plus faithful Faith, bringing up the rear like a pack animal.

Self-conscious despite her best attempts not to be, Cathy brushed at the dirty knees of her overalls.

Laurel bestowed upon them a thin-lipped smile and regal nod. "Good morning, ladies."

"Hey," Gwen said flatly, regarding the bridesmaids with a baleful eye. She was the only one of the Heartbroken who hadn't been asked to be a part of Laurel's wedding party. Her height and bulk had disqualified her from consideration.

Which said it all about Laurel Barnard, Cathy thought, turning her back to quickly finish the border of paper flowers. She did not want to get into it with Laurel—even though she knew she'd have to eventually make it clear that they were no longer in cahoots.

"Cathy?" Laurel said, too nicely.

Cathy didn't look up from gathering debris, but she made a noncommittal acknowledgement. "Mmm?"

Laurel put a hand out. Faith passed forward a clipboard.

"Ahem." Laurel paused to build the drama. "I finally got a copy of the sign-up list for the bachelor auction."

The bridesmaids clucked like hens.

"And guess who's on it."

The bridesmaids made questioning sounds.

"Zachary 'Heartbreak' Brody," Laurel said importantly. She gave a little shake of the head. "Of all the nerve."

At least one of the bridesmaids emitted a low-level *grrr.*

Cathy bunched the paper bag of litter in one hand. She capped the glue and slipped it into her canvas tote bag. "So what?"

"Yeah," Gwen said, scooting off the stage. "So what? Zack almost always signs up for the bachelor auction. Sister Mary Francis Floyd makes him. He's the biggest moneymaker they've got, and this year the church is raising funds for a new roof."

Laurel made a gesture of dismissal. "That's not the point, Gwen."

Gwen set her hands on her ample hips and scowled.

Cathy steamed. "Then what is?" she asked curtly, though she knew she was going to be sorry.

Faced with an unusual amount of resistance, Laurel pasted a conciliatory expression on her face. "We've decided that it's time for Zack to get his comeuppance. The bachelor auction presents the perfect opportunity."

"*We've* decided?" said Allie, who up to then had been mopily silent.

"If you must nitpick." Laurel rolled her eyes. "*I've* decided. We do all remember who the wronged party is, don't we?" The posse murmured in agreement. "As the jilted bride, I believe it's within my rights to make a unilateral decision."

"Isn't there some question about where the blame lies?" Cathy said, glancing toward the booths. "Zack's been mentioning something about a letter. A missing letter. Do any of you know about it?" He and Fred were talking, now and then throwing hard stares at the gathering of women. Was it her imagination, or did both of them appear disgruntled?

"Oh, phooey on that," Laurel said, conveniently ignoring how flustered she'd been on the day of her confrontation with Zack. She had a way of narrowing the focus to only her own concerns. "Allie and Faith mentioned it to me, but, really, how do we even know this infamous and invisible letter exists?"

Cathy couldn't prove it beyond her solid belief in Zack. She looked at Gwen for help, who shook her head.

Cathy turned to Allie, Zack's closest friend among the Heartbroken.

Allie was digging the toe of her sneaker into the gravel of the parking lot, her eyes downcast. She looked incredibly uncomfortable. Almost...guilty.

Cathy's gaze went from Allie to Fred to Zack. Another triangle? It was becoming painfully obvious that the Wednesday-night calligraphers were not quite the jovial chums she'd believed them to be. Rivalry and resentment had been swirling below the surface, and Zack's return had brought it all back up.

"Here's the plan," Laurel said, when there was no further argument. "Zack's always the prize of the bachelor auction. *Some* of us—" she arched a supercilious brow "—save all year for the chance to buy a date with Heartbreak. What a terrible irony."

Gwen flushed. "What about you, Laurel? You bought him for three straight years, even though he was going with Julia at the time—"

"That was for fun." Laurel's lips tightened. "And charity. Daddy wanted to give a large donation to the church."

"Sure, sure," Gwen said. "And you were forced to ace the rest of us out of the running."

Laurel tossed her hair. "The point is, this year none of us—not a single soul—shall bid on Zack. Imagine his humiliation then." She nearly chortled with wicked glee. "From Prince Charming to social outcast in the space of a year! He'll finally know what a mistake it was to treat me with such disrespect."

The bridesmaids *did* chortle—approvingly.

Cathy was astounded. Immediately, she knew she'd take no part in Laurel's campaign of ill will.

Laurel zeroed in on her. "And this goes for you, too,

Cathy. You, in particular. When no one else bids, Zack will look for you, as the recent object of his fickle affection, to come through for him. And you simply must not do it."

"Cripes, that's mean," breathed Allie.

Laurel swung on her. "You were all for us setting Cathy up with Zack in the first place. This is the payoff."

Allie recoiled. "I never wanted it to be so public."

"Tit for tat!" Laurel spat.

The bridesmaid posse echoed her vitriol, except Faith, who hung even farther back, looking miserable.

"You'll never get every single woman in town to agree," said Gwen. "*Someone* will bid."

Laurel simpered. "I've been working on it, and so have Liz, Kelly and Karen." The bridesmaids gloated. "Between us, we're friendly with every likely bidder. They've all agreed. Zack will be given the cold shoulder. This year, he's going to go begging."

Cathy closed her eyes for a moment. She was thoroughly appalled. And what was even more terrible was knowing that the scheme they'd hatched at Scarborough Faire only ten or so days ago had ballooned into such nastiness. She had to accept her share of the blame. If she hadn't been too wimpy and self-conscious to come clean at the start about her personal reasons for wanting Zack, this wouldn't have happened. At least not with her involvement.

Cathy gathered herself to speak, but it was Gwen who blurted, "What about Sister Mary Francis Fl—"

"I'll make a hefty donation to the church." Laurel sighed with irritation. "They won't lose any money on the deal."

"This is incredible," Allie said. "Laurel, you're just—"
Laurel cocked her head to stare her down.

Allie's voice quit in midstream. Strangely, she looked at Faith with panic in her eyes. "I have to go," she said suddenly. "The parade starts soon." She scurried away, leaving behind her staple gun and other supplies.

"I think we can count Allie in. Even though she hasn't bid on Zack in years." Laurel looked at Cathy and batted her lashes as if she weren't as low as a snake in the grass. "You'll go along, too, I'm certain, once you've realized your precarious standing with *Heartbreak*."

"Where's Julia?" Gwen muttered. "She'd put a stop to this."

Inwardly, Cathy was clinging to the emotional intimacy making love with Zack had given her. It gave her the strength to be firm. "Don't fool yourself, Laurel. I have no intention of—"

"Then we need to talk in private." Laurel grabbed Cathy by the elbow and hustled her away from the others. She was less delicate than appearances suggested—her fingers were like pincers. "It's you who'll end up the fool, Cathy. That's a given." Laurel let go and smoothed her hair over her shoulders. "You *know* his reputation."

"He's dated a lot," Cathy said, rubbing her arm. Her old insecurities reared up inside her and she struggled to keep them at bay. "There's nothing so terrible about that."

"Not to the woman at the head of the line," Laurel allowed. "But you'll be singing another tune when you wind up on the discard pile."

"If he's so awful, why did you want to marry him?"

"I was..."

Cathy crossed her arms and waited. Would Laurel tell the truth?

"Mistaken," she said. Her eyes shifted. "I thought he was worthy of being my husband, but I was mistaken."

"You were with Adam first, weren't you? But then Julia and Zack broke up. And you decided not to settle for second best."

Laurel inhaled sharply. "Who told you that? Julia? Zack?"

"You did," Cathy said. "Just now."

"None of that matters," Laurel insisted with what might almost be called an air of relief. But her face was drained of all color.

"What I can't figure out is how you managed to get to Zack after all those years of trying. From what I've heard, you were after him from the start and he was never interested."

Laurel quivered with outrage.

"And then suddenly," Cathy said, "you're planning the wedding of the decade. In approximately one month's time. How remarkable."

"What are you insinuating?"

"Nothing," Cathy said. She wouldn't break Zack's confidences. "Just wondering out loud."

"You think you're smart. But you're only a drab little mouse. I tried to help you out—" Laurel ran her gaze over Cathy's Indian-print head scarf, smudged glasses, baggy overalls and huaraches "—for all the good it did. See how long you can hold Zack's interest dressed like that."

Cathy withdrew, shaking her head in pity. "It's not clothes that make the woman, but whatever you say."

Laurel became shrill. "He's faithless. Sooner or later, he'll dump you."

Cathy kept walking.

"If you bid during the auction, I'll tell him everything!"

Cathy faltered, but only momentarily.

"He'll hate you, too, then!"

And Laurel would know, Cathy thought, ignoring her worry as well as the bridesmaid posse who swarmed toward Laurel, all atwitter. She set her sights on Zack and kept on walking. She'd come so far. She could go that little bit extra.

"NAW," FRED SAID. "I don't hate you 'cause you're bee-yew-ti-ful."

Zack laughed uncomfortably as he switched his cap around so the visor wouldn't be in the way when he leaned down to hammer in the stakes. "That's not what I meant."

"Sure it was. But don't worry, man. I got used to your pretty mug hogging all the attention way back in college. I know I'm a schlub." Fred slammed a hammer against a post that was already nailed in place. "Didn't think till now that it bothered Allie."

"Hey, c'mon. Allie and I kissed a couple times when we were kids—that's all. Innocent stuff. You're the one she married. That means a lot more than a childhood crush."

"Then why's she been carrying a torch for you all these years? And how come I didn't know it?" Fred swung the hammer again. It bounced off a knot in the raw wood. "Aw, hell."

"What did Allie say?"

"At first she said I was imagining things. All she felt for you was friendship. But then we kinda fought about it and finally—" Fred shrugged. "She admitted she's always been jealous of your girlfriends."

Zack squinted his eyes shut and cocked his face toward the sun. Within seconds its heat was sizzling on his skin, drying the sweat on his forehead and shoulders and chest. Sounds of construction, genial arguments, teasing laughter and footsteps crunching over gravel filled the air. He concentrated on the sunshine and the summery scent of lush wildflowers and resinous pine trees, hot sand and pungent lake water. The constriction in his chest gradually eased.

He took a deep breath, one of few he'd managed since yesterday when he'd begun to doubt Cathy's involvement. Thanks to Allie's revelation. Was that her intention?

"Did you make up to her?" he asked Fred.

"Sorta. Much as we could."

Zack lifted off his shades and wiped across his eyes and nose with the back of his wrist. "She loves you."

"Yeah, but it's not the same as it was." Fred shambled around the booth, looking it over. "Well, what are ya gonna do? We're married. That ain't gonna change."

"Of course not."

Fred stopped and posed, sucking in his gut. "Guess I'll go on a diet. Maybe start working out. Even if I'll never be an Adonis like you."

Together, he and Zack lifted the last brace and hammered it into place. "Allie doesn't want an Adonis."

"Yeah, well, she said she needs more attention."

"There you go. Do something romantic for her."

Fred squinted. "Like what?"

"What did you do when you two were first dating?"

"Brought her pizza and beer." Fred guffawed. "Looks like we haven't changed so much after all."

"Heck, no wonder she's tired of it."

"I don't have your smooth moves, Heartbreak. I'm a pizza-and-beer kind of man."

"Fine, then. Bring her pizza and beer. But use your imagination in the way you do it."

"Naked?" said Fred. "Should I bring it to her naked?"

Zack started laughing at the obtuse single-mindedness of the male gender.

Fred didn't get it. "Naked's romantic."

"You need to listen to Allie's hints. Think subtlety. A buck naked man is not subtle."

"Uh. Okay. I guess I could wear the leopard-print underwear she bought me for Valentine's Day."

Zack managed to stifle further laughter as he climbed up to weave an armful of leafy branches into the roof of the booth. All along the edges of the parking lot, similar booths were already finished. Right on time. A second wave of cars and trucks had begun to arrive—the vendors and craftpersons, looking to set up shop. Soon the Founder's Day festival would be in full swing. The events would continue throughout the day, culminating in a fireworks display over the lake.

From Zack's lofty position, he spotted Cathy at work over by the stage. She, Allie and Gwen seemed cheerful enough, but the mood evaporated when Laurel approached. Zack couldn't hear what was said, but he sensed the tension and he sure as shootin' could read their body language.

He jumped down beside Fred. "Look over there."

"Holy man, that's the bridesmaid posse. You better make a run for it, Heartbreak."

Zack didn't move. "Gonna tell me what's going down?"

Fred frowned at him. "Who says I know?"

"Allie's in it up to her eyebrows. She admitted as much, the other day after dinner."

Fred shrugged and turned away, but Zack saw the covert glances he threw over his shoulder while he busied himself doing nothing. Finally he relented. "Here's what

I know. Laurel's been lookin' for revenge and Cathy Timmerman was available for service. The gals dressed her up and sicced her on you."

Zack's voice went cold. "To what purpose?"

"That I don't know." Fred nudged Zack. "Some hardship, huh, having a willing lady laid at your feet?" He looked over at Cathy in her overalls. "Better send her back to Laurel before you take advantage of the offer. Looks like she's suffering a relapse."

Zack ignored him. He trusted Cathy—insofar as their personal relationship went. It was Laurel's involvement that was raising his hackles. That she would still be seeking revenge in spite of the circumstance was simply insupportable. "Seems like Laurel's getting shot down," he said. Cathy's stance screamed defiance. Good for her.

"I tried to warn ya. The broad holds a grudge."

"I'm not the guilty party. At least not wholly."

Suddenly Fred got extra busy packing up. "Well, yeah," he mumbled, "that's something Allie's gonna talk to you about."

"Allie? What do you mean?"

"Y'know how I told you we had it out? I learned more than I bargained for. Allie broke down and confessed. So I told her she had to make it right before things would be okay between us. Me dancin' around in a leopard-print sling won't solve everything."

Zack took off his cap and scratched at his prickly scalp. "I still don't get you. You're hinting that *Allie* had something to do with the cancelled wedding?"

"That's for her to say." Fred gave a hasty salute and took off into the growing crowd. "I'll look for you in the bachelor auction," he called over his shoulder. "There's bound to be fireworks when you come up for bid."

"That's for sure," chimed in another of the men who'd

been working on the booths. A group of them laughed good-naturedly.

Zack took the subsequent ribbing in stride. Though he'd managed to avoid the Founder's Day bachelor auction altogether for the past few years, Sister Mary Francis Floyd had called him a week ago and pinned him down with that sweet, steely manner of hers. One benefit of last year—he wouldn't have to worry about Laurel buying him this time around.

Thank God for small favors.

THE ADMIRAL hailed Cathy, stopping her in her tracks before she could get to Zack. She managed a glimpse of him waving at Fred Spangler, then joining a group of joshing men. An ice-cream truck trundled by. Cathy turned reluctantly to her father.

"Who on earth is that woman?" he said, indicating Kay Estress with a stiff jerk of his head. Kay was in charge of the parking, efficient as ever. "She darn near accosted me for choosing my own parking spot."

"That's Kay Estress. Didn't I mention her? She sold me the shop. She's—"

"She's a harridan!"

Cathy hushed him as her matchmaking abilities took an ignominious tumble. "I take it that means you don't like her?"

"Like her?" The Admiral snorted. "The woman could peel steel off the hull of a ship with her bare hands. She latched onto me like a leech and started ordering me about, telling me where to set up the parking cones...."

Cathy managed to keep her face blank while the Admiral went on about Kay, using words like *officious* and *abrupt* and *humorless* without realizing he might as well have been describing himself. She peeped over his shoulder now and then, searching for Zack, but he seemed to have disappeared. The Jag was parked nearby, though, surrounded by a gaggle of impressed ten-year-olds, so he couldn't have gone far.

"Women shouldn't be hard as nails," her father concluded. "They should be soft and round. Like your mother. Can we get out of here now—before that awful woman returns?"

Cathy gave up on finding Zack. "Yes, Mom was soft," she said, linking her arm with her father's. She remembered very little of her mother except that she'd been soft and warm and huggable. "Say, Dad, did I tell you how happy I am that you decided to visit? Even though you might have called first," she chided.

"I'm a man of action," her father boasted, then went on to reminisce about the admirable qualities of his curvaceous, soft-spoken wife while they walked to the car. Cathy wondered if it was age and retirement that had relaxed his abrupt manner...or was it her own maturing perspective?

The parking lot was a flurry of activity, with people and vehicles coming and going. Cathy wanted to go and open up shop while the costume parade proceeded down Central Street. She intended to close for the afternoon, go home to shower and change, and then hopefully hook up with Zack at the continuing festivities. He'd have to keep till then.

And that way, she'd have time to think of how to explain herself.

She wasn't betting on him remembering his fifth-grade pity pal, Cathy Beachball.

12

Zack bought Cathy a hot dog and an orange drink in the late afternoon since she'd missed the barbecue. It wasn't an ideal situation for an outpouring of confidences. They gobbled the food standing up, both of them a bit frazzled around the edges by the day's raucous events. Constant interruptions by garrulous townsfolk stopping by to say hello limited their own conversation to starts and stops.

On stage, Kay Estress was in the process of winning the Battleaxe pageant. She was dressed in dingy gray gingham-check skirts and Cathy's stained work apron, with her hair frizzed wildly out around her head. She carried a broom and stabbed it about the stage in sync with a string of shrewish commands.

"I didn't know Kay had such a theatrical streak," Cathy commented. She took a big bite of the liberally slathered hot dog.

With his paper napkin, Zack dabbed at the dot of mustard on her lip. "Stick around for a few years. You'll discover all kinds of hidden talents among us."

"I wasn't planning on going anywhere. In fact—"

Admiral Bell strode up to them, collar stiff, posture stiffer. "I've had enough of this tomfoolery."

Cathy smiled determinedly. The sun glinted off her dark glasses. "But doesn't Kay make a swell Battleaxe?"

The Admiral scoffed. "Pure nonsense." He eyed Zack.

"You're a pretty boy, just like my daughter's first husband. Don't tell me you go in for this folderol, too."

Zack blinked. "Her *first* husband?" Was that the Admiral's way of giving her *next* husband the stamp of approval?

"He means Chad, that's all," Cathy said, blushing.

Zack broke the awkward pause with a laugh. "I'll have to disappoint you, sir." He was unapologetic. "I sure did sign up for the bachelor auction." Cathy made a choking sound. "Didn't I mention that to you, Cath? It's for a good cause."

"So I heard." She coughed. The Admiral pounded her on the back, a cure worse than the symptom. By the time they were sorted out again, the subject was dropped, so thankfully Zack didn't have to explain his star bachelor status to a man who already thought all civilians were sissies or pantywaists.

The Admiral soon moved on. But then Fred and Allie wandered by, exhaustedly herding their brood ahead of them. They stopped to exchange a few words. Allie and Cathy spoke briefly. Zack thought he heard the word *bid*, but Fred was talking about arranging a game of pickup basketball against their rivals, the Collery cousins, so he couldn't be sure. Allie hefted a sleeping child in her arms, managing to avoid eye contact. In spite of Fred's previous assertion, she didn't look eager to confess.

Little Lucy hung on Zack's leg, begging to be picked up. He wound up carrying her to the Spangler's van, and when he returned Cathy had wandered off beyond the boundaries of the carnival. She stood in the long grass among the Queen Anne's Lace and purple phlox, staring at Mirror Lake, her back to the crowd.

"Hey," he said, coming up behind her.

She took his hand. "Come with me."

They walked through the sand to the tall lifeguard's chair. "Privacy," Cathy said as she kicked off her sandals. "Of a sort." She climbed with limber grace, her legs bare and lightly tanned beneath a colorful print skirt. The humid breeze billowed her loose blouse, giving him a glimpse of her flat abdomen, the round undersides of her breasts. His brain shut down—just for an instant— while all the blood and heat in his body surged south.

"Come on up." Cathy looked down at him with her sunglasses at the end of her nose and her dark ponytail swinging against one pink cheek. "There's room for both of us."

He took a quick look around. A few kids splashed in the water or played in the sand, but most of the crowd milled around the parking lot. The sound of the lake lapping at the shore reduced the noise to a mild roar.

He scaled the tower. Cathy scooted over. "Nice up here," she said, flicking aside her ponytail. Her hair was pulled straight back from her face in a sleek style that showed off her profile. She removed her sunglasses. Wincing at the glare, she made a small movement with her lower lip that made him remember a summer long ago and a girl he'd never forgotten...

Soon enough, he thought. Soon she'd trust him completely. Soon he'd hand her his heart.

They were pressed together in the chair. He put his arm around her slim waist. She leaned her head against his shoulder. "How much am I going to have to fork over?"

He hadn't recovered full brain function. "Pardon?"

"The bachelor auction. I'm guessing you're going to cost me a bundle."

He grimaced. "Oh, that. Don't bother. You can have

me anytime you want. Twenty-four hours a day." He slid his hand under her shirt to stroke her waist. "And all for free."

She elbowed him in the ribs. "You think I'm letting some other girl get you?"

"It's the body that's up for sale. Not the heart."

"Oh, yeah, that makes me feel lots better," she said, with exaggerated sarcasm.

They laughed.

"Call me greedy," she said, "but I need the body, too. I want the total package."

He put his mouth near her ear. *"Greedy."*

"Zack?" Her lashes dipped. "You know I'm teasing, right?"

"Right. You don't love me because I'm bee-yew-ti-ful."

She pretended to consider it carefully. "Well, not for that reason alone."

He tightened his grasp on her waist. She snuggled against his chest. For the moment, Zack thought, disregarding those questions that remained unanswered, his life couldn't get any better than this. It was a perfect summer day. Beauty all around. Sunshine danced over the water, striking gold sparks off the rippled surface. After a year of turmoil, he had found himself a new direction. He was aiming for a home and a life that was both the same and altogether new.

"We're okay," Cathy said.

He hesitated for the smallest instant. "Absolutely."

"You're sure?"

"I'm sure."

"Even if..." She pressed her face against him, her head tucked beneath his chin. "Even if I haven't been totally honest with you."

One last nagging doubt had returned for an instant, then vanished. *Poof.* "It doesn't matter," he said, and suddenly understood it to be true. Even if Cathy had partnered up with Laurel to some extent, that didn't change their feelings or what he knew was right. They'd known each other, maybe even been destined for each other, long before this.

"I've decided to believe in destiny," he said, and kissed her. She tasted sugary and tangy and when she teased his lips with her tongue he opened his mouth and drew her into himself until his lungs were bursting with heat and pleasure and a love so bright and pure it hurt. It hurt to breathe. It hurt to move. But it didn't hurt at all to say "I love you" with his lips moving against hers so the words were shared between them like a secret.

Cathy touched his face with her fingertips. Her eyes glistened. "I had so much to say, and now it seems that none of it matters." She shook her head as if to clear it. "It's all so tangled. I haven't been able to make sense of it. But I know—I know—" She stopped and wet her lips with her tongue and that made him want to kiss her again.

"I was going to explain," she said after they broke apart a second time.

"Shh. I already know. I know even more than you suspect."

She nodded, somewhat doubtfully.

"And I want you to hear the entire story about the wedding, too. It's not as bad as you think, but I won't keep protecting Laurel. Not when she has no conscience about carrying out her spiteful vendetta."

Cathy's face dropped. "Oh, gosh, *Laurel*." She grabbed a fistful of his shirt. "You don't know what she's planning. All just to hurt you. It won't work—I won't let it work. But—"

He put his arms around her. Hugged her tight. "It's okay."

"Laurel wants to hurt you."

"She won't. Nothing she can do will hurt me."

"I won't let it happen," Cathy vowed.

"My heroine," he said and then he kissed her again.

THE SKY was a dusky blue. The sun was hidden behind the tall pine trees, throwing deep shadows across the sand beach and up onto the graveled parking area. It wasn't dark yet, but Quimby's three-man police department had set up a couple of their portable lights to better illuminate the stage.

Gwen and Kay—still dressed as the Battleaxe—were having a high old time putting on the bachelor auction. Cathy had a seat toward the front of the crowd. She'd been poised on the edge of her chair for the past hour, but apparently Zack Brody was going to be the *pièce de résistance* of the event. Big surprise.

She'd discovered that a Quimby bachelor auction was not quite what she'd expected. The entire community participated. Males of all ages, sizes and even marital status had been put on the block. They were purchased by anyone with a few dollars, or—in a few instances— mere change to spare, though single women were quick to snatch up the most eligible of the participants.

"Here's Zack," said Julia, straightening up. Cathy had told her of Laurel's plan and they'd conspired to negate it. Even if no one else chimed in, they would top each other's bids until they'd reached a respectable amount. They'd thought that Allie might join in, but she'd made herself scarce.

The murmuring of the crowd grew to an excited buzz. "I have butterflies," Cathy said. This was strange to her, intentionally putting herself in the spotlight. *Only for Zack,* she thought.

Julia strained to get a glimpse of Laurel and her cronies, who were seated in the first row, at the far left.

Gwen introduced Zack in her booming voice. "And here's our final bachelor for the evening, a man we all know and love..." She stopped to aim a gloating smile at Laurel. "Ladies and gentlemen, I give you—" deep breath "—*Zachary 'Heartbreak' Brody!*"

There was an instant of total silence. Cathy's heart contracted into a chunk of ice.

Then Julia stood up and started to clap. Self-consciously, Cathy hopped up, dutifully adding her share to the applause. Soon others joined in, the applause picking up in enthusiasm as it grew. A few guys at the back of the crowd started a chant: "Heartbreak, Heartbreak, Heartbreak." Another contingent responded with a smattering of boos.

The audience stirred. Faces turned back and forth, gauging the different camps. Cathy felt gazes intent upon her. Heard the whispers. She slunk down into her seat.

"Settle down now," Gwen said.

Kay stepped up with her broom and her scowl. She batted at Zack's rear end. "Get along, you scoundrel!" she said, playing the Battleaxe a little too realistically. "Dang men are nuttin' but no-good varmints!" she railed at the crowd. A few jeers rang out. Others clapped and hooted in agreement.

Looking at Zack, Cathy forgot both the audience and herself. He had a confidence and easy grace that was simply beyond her ken. Even though the air was thick with tension and avid expectancy, he walked forward with a smile on his handsome face and his hands stuck casually in his pockets as if this was a Sunday afternoon stroll in the park. He was...he was...

He was her man.

And she was going to stake her claim in the most public way possible.

Gwen had opened the bidding while Cathy was absorbed in her own thoughts. When no one jumped in, Gwen asked again. And again. The silence and tension grew thicker. In the front row, Laurel tipped up her chin with an air of smug victory.

Julia nudged Cathy. She jerked herself back to attention, then gripped the chair in front of her as she slowly got to her feet. The young woman seated in it turned to stare, which was nothing compared to Laurel's white-hot glare when she saw that Cathy had risen and intended to speak.

"Do we have any bids?" Gwen pleaded.

From the elevated stage, Zack looked at Cathy and smiled. She gave him a little wave, her heart overflowing.

"We need a bid," prompted Gwen.

I can do this, Cathy thought, taking a swift survey of the audience. Every eye was trained on her. The buoyant joy of knowing Zack loved her did not prevent the attention from being excruciating. She closed her eyes for a brief moment, sucked in a shaky breath, then blinked several times before focusing solely on Zack.

He was her man. Hers alone.

She opened her mouth, but her vocal cords were frozen.

"Three dollars and seventy-two cents," called a rusty

female voice, coming from the midst of a loose knot of bystanders who hadn't been able to find a seat.

"Eh?" A questioning sound floated from Cathy's parted lips.

On stage, Gwen seemed flummoxed. "Three dollars? And seventy-two cents? For *Zack Brody?*"

A vindictive cackle came from the direction of the bridesmaid posse.

"That's all I've got." The silent, watchful crowd began to buzz again as a wizened, white-haired woman in threadbare clothing stepped to the front. She was fingering through a change purse. "Three dollars and seventy-two cents," the old lady repeated, quite satisfied with the bid. "I wouldn't spend it on the rest of these clowns, but this fella's worth it."

Reggie Lee Marvin came forward, holding up a coin. "Here's another nickel, Ma. I found it on the ground."

A wave of laughter rolled through the crowd.

Zack merely nodded. "Thank you," he said to the woman.

Cathy's knees gave out. "Huh?" she said as she plopped onto her chair.

"That's Emmie Marvin," Julia explained. "Reggie Lee's mother. They live in that little tar-paper shacky place at the edge of town. For her, three bucks plus change is one heck of an impressive bid."

Cathy blinked. "She knows Zack?"

"One summer, he and Adam rebuilt her little house. Put in new insulation and windows, mended the leaky roof."

"Oh. Wow."

"We have a bid of three dollars and seventy-two cents," Gwen said questioningly.

"Seventy-seven cents," Reggie Lee corrected. More laughter.

Another woman popped up—a middle-aged homely sort who rarely spoke up, but was suddenly saying in a clear, ringing voice, "I'll bid ten dollars." She was someone Cathy had seen around town, but never met, one of those unassuming people who quietly go about their business without notice. Cathy was willing to bet that *Zack* had noticed.

Laurel and her posse put their heads together. "Losers," one of them said.

A hand waved. "Twenty-five dollars!" called a very plump young woman from the back of the crowd. She ignored the insult when a group of young guys in basketball jerseys and baggy shorts fell all over themselves, snickering and cat-calling in disbelief. "Twenty-five dollars," she said firmly. "No, make that fifty."

"Uh, I don't think you can bid against yourself," Gwen said from the stage. She looked around for support. "Can she?"

"Sixty!" someone called.

A tall, gaunt woman stood up. Miss Cora Selverstone, the spinster librarian. "I will put in a bid of seventy-five dollars," she said, even though she was known for her severe frugality. She took in a few of the gaping expressions. "He's a fine young man. Worth every penny."

"Eighty," said a small voice at the front.

Laurel shot to her feet, enraged. "You wouldn't!"

Faith's blond head bowed, then lifted. "I would. I do." She cleared her throat. "I bid eighty."

"Ninety," the plump girl called. "That's all I have."

"Too rich for my blood," Miss Selverstone said, and sat down.

"Ninety-two," Faith responded, fumbling in her purse.

Laurel whirled to confront the crowd. "This is wrong."

The buzz magnified. "One hundred," another woman called triumphantly, ignoring Laurel. She waved a wad of cash. "I've got one hundred!"

Cathy leapt to her feet. She'd been told that the bids rarely topped a hundred, so it was lucky she'd brought her checkbook. "One-fifty," she said in a voice so strong it silenced the gathering. Numerous heads in the audience turned toward her as if they were watching a tennis match and she'd just aced the opponent. A sprinkling of applause became a torrent.

Zack was clapping, too, and at the sight of him Cathy broke into a big, bashful smile.

"Whew." Gwen wiped her brow. "Okay, quiet down, folks. We've got a bid of one hundred and fifty dollars from Cathy Timmerman. Anyone else?"

"One fifty-five," Julia bid, laughing when Cathy kicked her.

Two women were conferring. "One-eighty," they called together.

"Kelly!" Laurel screeched. "Karen! You promised!"

"Sorry," the twins said, not sounding the least bit sorry.

"Okay, that's one-hundred and eighty from the Thompson twins," Gwen said, to the accompaniment of a wolf whistle from the back of the crowd. She looked stunned. Zack looked stunned. Laurel looked very, very angry, which wasn't a good look for her.

Cathy had forgotten about the crowd. "Two hundred."

Zack waved off further bids. "Okay, that's enough, now. This is getting out of hand."

Gwen had recovered herself. "Who's going to give me two-ten?" she bellowed.

A woman in a sophisticated suit bid, "Two-ten," with a discreet twitch of one bejeweled finger. She simpered. "Why not?"

"Oh, boy," Cathy muttered. "Who's that?"

Julia was craning to see, along with everyone else. "I think it's the Bailey's rich cousin. Just visiting. You might be in trouble." She waved. "Hey. Think I see Allie, way at the back."

Cathy took a deep breath. "Two-fifty!"

The other woman got a stubborn look. "Two-seventy-five!"

"Three hundred," Cathy said at once, trying to sound unbeatable. A few more bids and she'd be digging into her savings.

"Three-twenty-five," the other woman said, not quite as enthusiastically.

Cathy swallowed, prepared to bid again. Before she could, a male bidder took charge, shouting out an amount— "Seven hundred and fifty dollars and not a penny more!" —that elicited a few shocked exclamations and then a great cheer.

"Seven hundred and fifty," Gwen shouted above the clamor. "Going...going...*gone!* For a record price, Zack Brody goes to..."

Cathy slapped a hand over her gaping mouth.

"...Admiral Wallace Winston Bell, U.S. Navy, retired!"

THE CROWD was milling, but not many were dispersing. Julia and Cathy made their way toward the gaily decorated stage, where the Admiral was writing out a check to Sister Mary Francis Floyd, who was alternating between hugging Zack, Gwen, Kay and then Zack again. The enthusiastic nun would have hugged the Admiral, too, but he'd stepped back in alarm.

Cathy felt shaky. People were smiling at her, calling out their congratulations. Someone made a comment about Laurel's daddy finally being outbid. A few women, those who'd obviously sided with Laurel, looked seriously miffed.

As for Laurel herself, she was lost amidst a group of women, but her voice could be heard trilling up and down the scale as she decried the traitorous bidding.

Transaction complete, the Admiral locked a hand at the back of Zack's neck and towed him over to Cathy as if he was a reluctant suitor at a shotgun wedding. "Here you go, girl. He's all yours."

She giggled at the sheer absurdity. "Gee, for me, Dad? You really shouldn't have."

"Thought you wanted him."

"Oh, I do." She blinked several times, trying to keep from crying. "Yes. I want him." She reached her hands toward Zack's.

"Just wait and see how much good it'll do you," Laurel said, suddenly amongst them. She was thin-lipped with anger. "I rather doubt that the smooth operator will appreciate knowing how we turned the tables on him."

She rounded on Zack. "That's right. Cathy's just a pawn. I've been using her to toy with you, but she's too spineless to extract a fitting conclusion."

Laurel stopped, breathing hard. "So, then. Let me do the honors," she said, and reared back to slap Zack in the face.

He caught her wrist. "Laurel. I told you not to try that

again. You don't want to make a scene. You've already sunk low enough."

"Not me," she retorted, fuming as she pulled out of his grasp. "I did nothing—"

"*It was me.*"

The onlookers stirred as Allie Spangler made her way past them. She stopped in front of Zack, her face as red as her hair. "It was me. My fault." Her body looked as tense and electric as a live wire, but she held herself very still with an enormous effort. Only her voice shook. "I'm sorry, but I took the letter you left for Laurel, cancelling the wedding. At first I only meant to read it, but then..." Unsuccessfully biting back a sob, she hung her head in shame.

"You?" Laurel said, her hard, waxen face melting in somewhat dramatic disbelief.

"I was...jealous. It wasn't fair that after all these years Zack picked—he picked Laurel—" Allie trembled. "I just couldn't believe it. *Laurel.* She's not nearly worthy— not by a long shot."

Laurel's jaw dropped at the blatant insult.

Julia stepped up beside Allie and slid an arm around her shoulder. She murmured in low tones.

But Allie wasn't finished. "I didn't mean for everyone to blame you. I put the letter underneath the silver bowl on the Barnards' foyer table."

"Why?" Zack asked.

"All Laurel talked about was her fancy wedding. She was planning it even before she was engaged, knowing she'd snare one of the Brody brothers. She didn't care about *you* as a person, Zack. So I thought—let her have the wedding. Without the groom." Another sob escaped, and Allie clapped a hand over her mouth. "I was sure they'd find the letter afterward," she muttered. "And you'd be in the clear."

Laurel's fingers curled into claws. She raised them threateningly. "You little bitch," she said in a low voice.

"Don't bother," Allie croaked. "You already know the truth because Faith told you. Recently, I think. She saw me with the letter that night, but she never said a word. Till now."

Laurel's jaw clenched.

"Faith?" someone from the crowd said. Emotion was running high. "Where's Faith Fagan?"

It was Reggie Lee Marvin who spoke up. "She's there, over there. She's the one who tore up the letter!"

Faith sat hunched in a folding chair, gripping her arms. She didn't speak.

"No," Laurel said. "No, not Faith. She wouldn't betray me like—" She halted abruptly, clearly remembering how Faith had gone against her instructions and bid for Zack. "Zack," Laurel said bitterly, swinging around again. "This is all Zack's fault."

"Nuh-uh," protested Reggie Lee. He rubbed his forehead, frowning with concentration. "It was Miss Faith. I was there, outside the window, trimmin' the rose bushes. She tore Mr. Zack's letter up into little bits and dropped 'em in the trash can. I tried to tell Mr. Barnard the next time I mowed, but he said I shouldn't start no more talk...."

All at once, the air seemed to go out of those who'd gathered around the staging area. By twos and threes, they pulled themselves together and left, murmuring about the stunning events in a subdued manner. For the moment, there didn't seem to be a lot left to say.

Even Laurel was deflated. Shoulders slumped in defeat, she walked away without another word.

Cathy turned slowly in a circle, trying to get her bearings. There were still plenty of people around, but many of them had moved toward their cars or the beach, preparing for the fireworks show. The Admiral marched off toward the beach, with Gwen, of all people, trotting at his side. They seemed surprisingly...friendly.

The stage lights made the night sky appear darker than it was, although the sun had nearly set. Feathery blue and gray clouds hung low on the western horizon, outlined in gold. Tiny stars had begun to appear overhead.

Zack was watching Cathy. He offered her a quick twitch of a smile that came and went in a heartbeat. His eyes were dark with sorrow.

She caught at her breath. "Oh, Zack."

"I wouldn't blame you if you're thinking I'm not such a prize after all." His voice was filled with regret, and he shook his head in wonder. "I've been so dense, thinking that I'd managed to play the field and not hurt anyone." His gaze followed Julia as she escorted a sniffling Allie away from the stage. "Allie," he said. "All these years. I didn't suspect."

Cathy went to him. She hugged him with her arms around his waist. He dropped his forehead against hers and sighed deeply. She said, "Don't, don't, don't," over and over again, and after a while the tension in him began to ease. He brushed a hand over her bottom. Touched his lips to her cheek.

"I've been hurt," she whispered, "but never by you. So don't say that ever again. I know you, Zack Brody, and I know this wasn't your fault."

"You know me?" he said quietly. "After ten days, you know me?"

Cathy thought of how she'd jumped into the quarry

pond. How she'd stood up and claimed Zack as her own. Third time's a charm, she told herself, and closed her eyes to take the plunge.

"No, Zack." Her voice cracked. "I've known you a lot longer than that."

13

"CATHY BEACHBALL," Zack said, standing in his backyard and looking up at the sky as navy blue darkened to black. "I don't remember that name at all. It's terrible."

He doesn't remember me. Cathy rubbed her prickling arms. *Of course he doesn't remember me. Why should he remember me?* She'd been in his life for one year. Yes, they'd been friends of a sort, but that was nearly two decades ago. Only a sentimental fool would cling to the past for so long.

They'd decided not to stay for the fireworks. Feeling fraught with emotion, she'd told him everything on the drive home—living with her grandparents, attending Quimby Elementary, the pain of being teased mercilessly, the pleasure of having one good friend, a boy named Zack who'd rescued her from utter despair....

And he didn't remember.

"No Cathy Beachball," he mused, and there were pinpoints of light glittering in his eyes. Or was that only a reflection of the stars?

His gaze dropped to her face. "But I do remember Cathy Bell."

She couldn't speak.

"And I recognize her, too."

My stars, she thought. *Oh, my stars.* "Y-you couldn't possibly..."

"Not right off the bat," he admitted. "A few times I

thought you seemed familiar. It wasn't until you mentioned your father's name, and I put the two together—Cathy Bell—that I knew for sure who you were. I remember your grandparents, even. How they used to chase us out of their garden."

"We were stealing strawberries," Cathy said in awe, memories coming in a rush. She'd been so happy that day. Zack had seen her outside when he'd ridden past on his bike on the way from the beach, and he'd stopped to talk. And stayed. They hadn't done much, just played cards, stole the strawberries and walked by the river, but she remembered the fruit as the sweetest she'd ever tasted and the sky so blue, and Zack, gangly and brown, happy-go-lucky, friendly as a puppy, even to her stern grandparents. She'd been a little bit in love with him ever since.

"I remember," he said. "I remember everything about you. I always wondered where you'd gone."

"My father came to get me at the end of the school year. I wanted to tell you I was leaving, but I was too shy to call. My gosh, I couldn't call a boy."

"I missed you," he said, so simply it melted her heart.

"No." It was too much to believe. "Really. Why would you miss me? I was only the chubby outcast you were being kind to."

Suddenly Zack was sweeping her into his arms. "That's not how I remember you, Cath."

"What do you remember?" she asked, breathless because he was squeezing her so hard.

"I remember a pretty girl with wire-rimmed glasses, quiet, with dark hair and big blue eyes. Serious eyes. She was plump, yep, but she had the smoothest skin, and the roundest cheeks when she smiled, like peaches. And she was so smart and talented—she could draw anything, even wicked caricatures of the kids who teased her for being unique. I remember that was why I liked her—she was her own person. She wasn't afraid to be different."

"I *was* afraid."

"Okay." He kissed her. "But you didn't change, did you?"

"Only because I couldn't. And then when I could—" Pressure built at the back of her eyes. She squeezed them shut. "I made a big mistake. I tried to be someone I'm not."

"'S okay," Zack whispered, his breath drying her wet lashes as they fluttered up and down.

"I didn't learn my lesson, either." She had to tell him everything, but this last bit was turning out to be harder than she'd thought. It was important that he know she could be as generous in spirit as he. "Zack. When I came to Quimby, it was partly to see you again. Maybe even mostly. Because I still remembered you. Then when Gwen found out you were coming back to town—"

"I know all about it. The 'Heartbroken' cooked up a scheme."

Cathy nodded. "They gave me a makeover. They told me to...seduce you. As if I could."

He smiled, a quick flare of heat making his eyes simmer. "You did fine."

"Actually." She cleared her throat. "I did more than fine. I wasn't supposed to sleep with you—"

"But you couldn't help it," he interrupted with a wicked grin.

She slapped his chest. "I was *supposed* to make you want me—"

"I wanted you from the start. Who thought up that window thing? That was really good."

"Oh, no," she said, feeling a blush working its way up her throat. "That part was a mistake."

He nuzzled her neck. "To err is woman."

"Wait, Zack." She pulled away from him and walked across the lawn to an iron bench that was set in the shelter of the drooping willow branches, its fancy white filigree delineated against a backdrop of dark glistening water. "I have to finish." She took a deep breath and sat, relaunching into her explanation. "I was supposed to make you crazy with desire and then cut you to the quick. Stab you with my rejection and let Laurel twist the knife, as it turns out. But I never intended to follow through with that last part. What I wanted was..." She took Zack's hand and drew him down beside her. "I wanted to make you fall in love with me."

Wordlessly, he brushed his knuckles across her cheek.

"But I realize now how impossible that is. You can't *make* someone love you."

"It happens on its own," he agreed. "Sometimes it's like a lightning strike. In other cases, it grows slowly over time until you realize that it's just there, that the other person is a crucial part of who you are." He took her chin in his hand. "I always wanted that."

She bit her lip, trying not to tremble. She sought his eyes. "I love you, Zack."

"I love you."

This is like drowning, she thought. But not dying. Somehow she'd survived and now was living in a rarefied realm. Breathing water. Awash in love.

"Look," Zack said as several popping sounds came from the distance. A few red and pink fireworks burst near the horizon, just above the tops of the willow trees. *Bang.* A huge and glittering purple chrysanthemum bloomed against the dark sky.

"I want to tell you about Laurel," Zack said, watching the fireworks.

"You don't have to. I trust you completely. What's done is done."

"Not in this case. Because I didn't do it."

She stared at his profile, lit by flashes of green and blue and white and red. "What does that mean?"

Finally he turned to look at her, a small smile playing about his mouth. "I didn't sleep with Laurel. I never even went out with her. The baby wasn't mine."

"How can that be?" she said in shocked wonder. "How...?" She looked at Zack's serious expression and then she knew. "Your brother. It was Adam's baby."

"That's what Laurel claimed. She came to me one day this past spring, said Adam had gotten her pregnant but was refusing to marry her. She seemed desperate. I believed her, which was my first mistake." He turned again to study the fireworks, a muscle jumping in his jaw. "I went to Adam, but he was defensive and hot-headed before I even got to ask him about it. We had a bad argument that didn't make a lot of sense, in retrospect. I didn't know it at the time, but Laurel had been playing us against each other."

"She wanted to marry you, not Adam. He was only her fall-back position."

Zack looked surprised. "Yeah, I guess that was it, more or less. Later I found out she'd told Adam that she'd slept with me, too, and that the baby was mine. If Adam and I had talked rationally instead of losing our tempers—" He sighed. "We could have spared everyone a lot of grief."

The whistling and popping sounds continued in the distance as the fireworks broke across the sky. Cathy curled her hands around Zack's and squeezed.

"Anyway, Adam left town the night of our fight. I had no choice but to bite the bullet and ask Laurel to marry me so the baby—if there ever really was a baby—would at least have the proper name."

"But then she miscarried. Or claimed to."

"I think it was real, and that I do regret. As did Adam, when he learned the truth. But of course I didn't want to marry Laurel after that. Except the wedding was planned, the invitations had gone out. Laurel pleaded with me..."

Cathy was outraged at the woman's gall. "She used your sense of honor against you."

Zack shook his head. "Guess I wasn't as honorable as she thought. When the word came that Adam had been in a car accident out in Idaho, I couldn't cancel the wedding fast enough. Maybe Laurel was suspicious, because she made up excuses not to see me, not to come to the phone. So I left the letter. And I never looked back."

Cathy bumped her shoulder against his. "It's over now. All over."

He gazed into her eyes. "And do you still love me?"

"Of course I do."

"I always knew I'd find you," he said in a husky whisper that sent a delicious thrill through her. "Laurel's like a bad dream now. You're the woman who was meant to be my bride."

She went all weak inside, but for once it was a good kind of weakness. Drowning in it, she thought. *I am drowning in love.* "I can hardly believe this."

"Believe it. Remember, your father already acquired me for you. I'm bought and paid for."

She ran her hands up his chest. His heart pounded beneath her palm. "It was one heck of a good deal."

"The Admiral obviously knows what he's doing."

"So do you." His hands had disappeared beneath her shirt.

She moved restlessly against him, her emotions melting into heat and lust. The clasp of her bra sprang apart and he caught her breasts in his hands as his mouth came down on hers. The possession in the kiss was darkly exciting. She tingled with it, as if sparks from the fireworks were raining over her skin.

He pulled her into his lap. Pushed her skirt up around her waist, his hands sliding over her bare thighs. "Can we?" she said. "Out here?"

He raised her loose blouse. "Everyone's at the fireworks," he muttered into the hot hollow between her breasts, his tongue licking a path from one breast to the other. He nipped at one of the budded peaks and she felt the contact like an electric shock, arching against him as the connection sizzled down through the center of her body. She pushed against his arousal, and was rewarded with his ragged gasp.

"Someone will see," she whispered.

"No. They can't see." The trees made a green curtain between them and the neighboring houses. "I want you, Cathy." He stroked his hand beneath her skirt, over the slick satin triangle of her bikini underpants. "I need you." A raspy chuckle. "Real bad."

"I can tell." She pressed a hand to the hard bulge beneath his fly, felt it jump beneath her touch. A quiet, solid sense of satisfaction grew inside her. *I did this*, she thought. *Me. Cathy Beachball.*

She threw back her head and smiled at the shimmering sky, its glorious explosions of sparkle and color becoming a part of her joy as she rocked her hips against Zack's lower body and felt the passion build between them.

He reached down to free himself, then pulled her even closer, his hot flesh finding hers as she opened her legs wider, surging against him as he tried to slip her panties down. He gave that up with a muttered oath and simply stretched the elastic to one side and pushed himself up into her, all of him at once, big and hard and deep.

The shout she let out was loud enough to rouse the neighbors. He captured her mouth, kissing away her shuddering shock at the sweet intrusion of his body thrusting into hers. Slowly she began to move against him, feeling weak again, her insides molten with desire, as liquid as warm syrup dripping down the side of a bottle.

"You didn't answer," Zack said, panting between each word as he drove rhythmically inside her. She heard his meaning in the timbre of his voice, but she swung her head forward to search his face all the same.

Their eyes locked. "Will you be my bride?" His grip tightened on her hips and she met his thrust in a rush of careening sensation.

She said yes. Threw back her head and shouted her yes at the exploding sky.

"It's—a—risky—proposition."

"No risk at all," she said, lost in the wonder of loving him, and making love with him, all pulsing heat and need and a passion so huge it filled her body, over-flowed onto his, flooding her senses so that she lost touch with every reality but Zack. She swayed with him, climaxing in a series of sumptuous waves that broke through her body like the surf, sweeping him into the strange swirling world where she breathed love, she breathed love, she breathed only love forever on end as the fireworks burst all around them in vivid plumes of glittering celebration.

Modern Romance™
...seduction and
passion guaranteed

Tender Romance™
...love affairs that
last a lifetime

Sensual Romance™
...sassy, sexy and
seductive

Blaze
...sultry days and
steamy nights

Medical Romance™
...medical drama on
the pulse

Historical Romance™
...rich, vivid and
passionate

MILLS & BOON®

Winner at

2001 IDEA INTERNATIONAL
DESIGN
EFFECTIVENESS
AWARDS

MILLS & BOON®

heat *of the* night

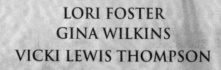

LORI FOSTER
GINA WILKINS
VICKI LEWIS THOMPSON

3 SIZZLING SUMMER NOVELS

Available at most branches of WH Smith,
Tesco, Martins, Borders, Eason, Sainsbury's
and most good paperback bookshops.

SANDRA MARTON

raising the stakes

When passion is a gamble...

Available from 19th April 2002

MILLS & BOON
FOREIGN AFFAIRS
A captivating 12 book collection of sun-kissed seductions.
Enjoy romance around the world.
DON'T MISS BOOK 9
latin liaisons–
Red-hot husband material...
Available from 7th June
Available at most branches of WH Smith, Tesco, Martins, Borders, Eason, Sainsbury's and most good paperback bookshops.
FA/RTL/9

FREE!
2 Books
and a surprise gift!

We would like to take this opportunity to thank you for reading this Mills & Boon® book by offering you the chance to take TWO more specially selected titles from the Sensual Romance™ series absolutely FREE! We're also making this offer to introduce you to the benefits of the Reader Service™—

- ★ FREE home delivery
- ★ FREE gifts and competitions
- ★ FREE monthly Newsletter
- ★ Books available before they're in the shops
- ★ Exclusive Reader Service discount

Accepting these FREE books and gift places you under no obligation to buy; you may cancel at any time, even after receiving your free shipment. Simply complete your details below and return the entire page to the address below. *You don't even need a stamp!*

YES! Please send me 2 free Sensual Romance books and a surprise gift. I understand that unless you hear from me, I will receive 4 superb new titles every month for just £2.55 each, postage and packing free. I am under no obligation to purchase any books and may cancel my subscription at any time. The free books and gift will be mine to keep in any case.

T2ZEB

Ms/Mrs/Miss/Mr ....Initials.................................
BLOCK CAPITALS PLEASE

Surname ....

Address...

....

....Postcode ....

Send this whole page to:
UK: The Reader Service, FREEPOST CN81, Croydon, CR9 3WZ
EIRE: The Reader Service, PO Box 4546, Kilcock, County Kildare (stamp required)

Offer not valid to current Reader Service subscribers to this series. We reserve the right to refuse an application and applicants must be aged 18 years or over. Only one application per household. Terms and prices subject to change without notice. Offer expires 30th August 2002. As a result of this application, you may receive offers from other carefully selected companies. If you would prefer not to share in this opportunity please write to The Data Manager at the address above.

Mills & Boon® is a registered trademark owned by Harlequin Mills & Boon Limited.
Sensual Romance™ is being used as a trademark.